POKÉMON™
TRAINER ACTIVITY BOOK:
FROM TRAINER TO CHAMPION!

PIKACHU PRESS™

$12.99 USA
$15.50 CAN

Publisher: Heather Dalgleish
Publishing Manager: Amy Levenson
Art Director: Eric Medalle
Designer: Hiromi Kimura
Writer: Lawrence Neves
Editor: Wolfgang Baur
Merchandise Development Director: Phaedra Long
Merchandise Development: Hank Woon
Project Manager: Emily Luty

The Pokémon Company International
601 108th Avenue NE Suite 1600
Bellevue, WA 98004 USA

Printed in Shenzhen, China
First printing August 2015.

This book was produced by Walter Foster Publishing, a division of Quarto Publishing Group USA Inc.
Walter Foster is a registered trademark.

ISBN: 978-1-60438-187-0

POKÉMON

TRAINER ACTIVITY BOOK:

FROM TRAINER TO CHAMPION!

TABLE OF CONTENTS

☁ WELCOME TO ☁ THE KANTO REGION

This is it Pokémon fans! The region where it all started. Kanto is filled with many of the Pokémon that we remember fondly, that start out every regional specialist's adventure, but can you recognize them all?

KANTO

JOHTO

HOENN

SINNOH

UNOVA

KALOS

KANTO

JOHTO

HOENN

SINNOH

UNOVA

KALOS

✿ FIRST PARTNER POKÉMON ✿

Let's start at the start! Can you identify these first partner Pokémon from just their silhouettes? One of these three that will join you at the start of your journey through Kanto!

1

2

3

WORD SEARCH

KANTO

JOHTO

HOENN

SINNOH

UNOVA

KALOS

Let's see how many Kanto region Pokémon you can identify. There are 150 Kanto Pokémon to find! Be careful— you'll find some Pokémon from other regions mixed in here!

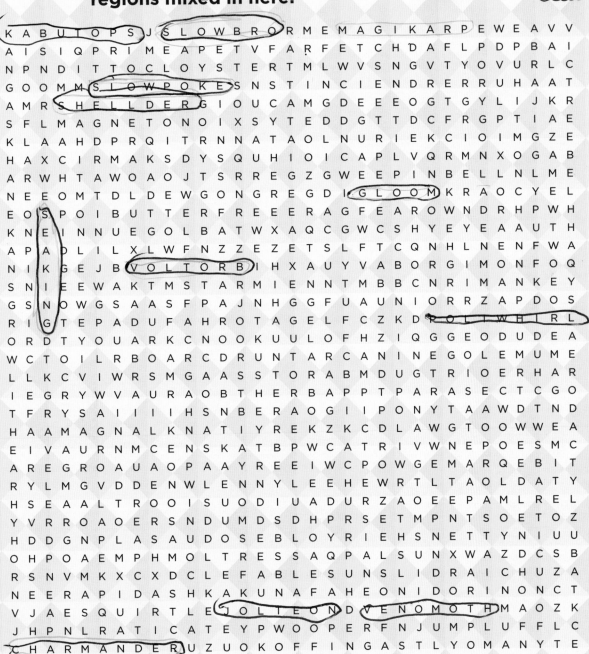

```
K A B U T O P S J S L O W B R O R M E M A G I K A R P E W E A V V
A I S I Q P R I M E A P E T V F A R F E T C H D A F L P D P B A I
N P N D I T T O C L O Y S T E R T M L W S N G V T Y O V U R L C
G O O M M S L O W P O K E S N S T I N C I E N D R E R R U H A A T
A M R S H E L L D E R G I O U C A M G D E E E O G T G Y L I J K R
S F L M A G N E T O N O I X S Y T E D D G T T D C F R G P T I A E
K L A A H D P R Q I T R N N A T A O L N U R I E K C I O I M G Z E
H A X C I R M A K S D Y S Q U H I O I C A P L V Q R M N X O G A B
A R W H T A W O A O J T S R R E G Z G W E E P I N B E L L N L M E
N E E O M T D L D E W G O N G R E G D I G L O O M K R A O C Y E L
E O S P O I B U T T E R F R E E E R A G F E A R O W N D R H P W H
K N E I N N U E G O L B A T W X A Q C G W C S H Y E Y E A A U T H
A P A D L I L X L W F N Z Z E Z E T S L F T C Q N H L N E N F W A
N I K G E J B V O L T O R B I H X A U Y V A B O R G I M O N F O Q
S N I E E W A K T M S T A R M I E N N T M B B C N R I M A N K E Y
G S N O W G S A A S F P A J N H G G F U A U N I O R R Z A P D O S
R I G T E P A D U F A H R O T A G E L F C Z K D R O L I W H I R L
O R D T Y O U A R K C N O O K U U L O F H Z I Q G G E O D U D E A
W C T O I L R B O A R C D R U N T A R C A N I N E G O L E M U M E
L L K C V I W R S M G A A S S T O R A B M D U G T R I O E R H A R
I E G R Y W V A U R A O B T H E R B A P P T P A R A S E C T C G O
T F R Y S A I I I I H S N B E R A O G I I P O N Y T A A W D T N D
H A A M A G N A L K N A T I Y R E K Z K C D L A W G T O O W W E A
E I V A U R N M C E N S K A T B P W C A T R I V W N E P O E S M C
A R E G R O A U A O P A A Y R E E I W C P O W G E M A R Q E B I T
R Y L M G V D D E N W L E N N Y L E E H E W R T L T A O L D A T Y
H S E A A L T R O O I S U O D I U A D U R Z A O E E P A M L R E L
Y V R R O A O E R S N D U M D S D H P R S E T M P N T S O E T O Z
H D D G N P L A S A U D O S E B L O Y R I E H S N E T T Y N I U U
O H P O A E M P H M O L T R E S S A Q P A L S U N X W A Z D C S B
R S N V M K X C X D C L E F A B L E S U N S L I D R A I C H U Z A
N E E R A P I D A S H K A K U N A F A H E O N I D O R I N O N C T
V J A E S Q U I R T L E J O L T E O N D V E N O M O T H M A O Z K
J H P N L R A T I C A T E Y P W O O P E R F N J U M P L U F F L C
C H A R M A N D E R U Z U O K O F F I N G A S T L Y O M A N Y T E
```

KANTO

JOHTO

HOENN

SINNOH

UNOVA

KALOS

⊙ IT TAKES ALL TYPES ⊙

You know your region, and you seem to know your Pokémon, so let's see if you know your Pokémon types. Match the Pokémon on the left with the types on the right. Be careful—some of the Pokémon are dual types.

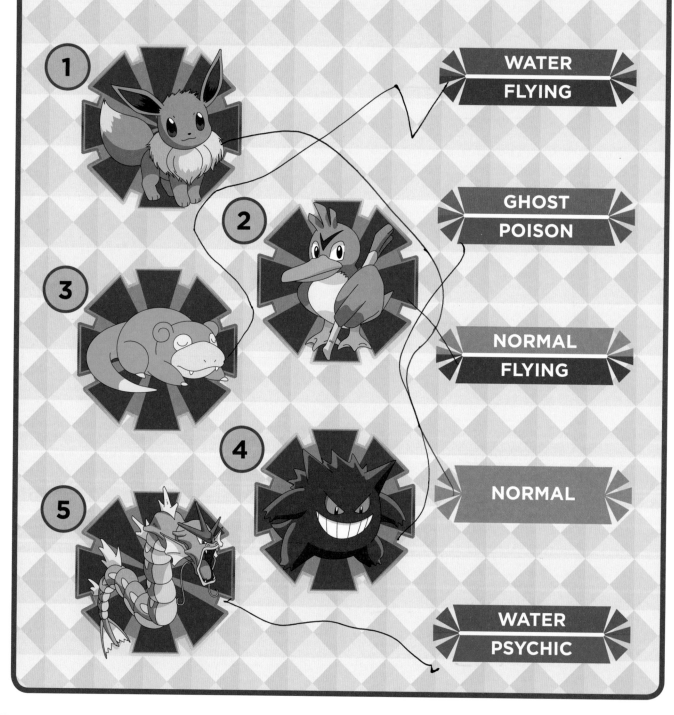

1

WATER
FLYING

2

GHOST
POISON

3

NORMAL
FLYING

4

NORMAL

5

WATER
PSYCHIC

ANSWER ON PAGE 103

KANTO

JOHTO

HOENN

SINNOH

UNOVA

KALOS

⊙ EVOLUTION REVOLUTION ⊙

You know your first partner Pokémon, but do you know their Evolutions? See if you can guess the correct order and fill in the numbers and names below.

3   4

6   2

5   1

Bulbasaur → (4) _____ → (3) _____

Charmander → (6) _____ → (1) _____

Squirtle → (2) _____ → (5) _____

⊙ KANTO REGION CROSSWORD ⊙

Figuring out Pokémon by region is perplexing. Let's test your knowledge by asking you a few questions about Pokémon of the Kanto region.

7. P I K A C H U

DOWN

1. As _ _ _ _ _'s pendulum swings and shines, anyone watching falls into a hypnotic trance. To enhance the effect, it always keeps the pendulum polished.

2. _ _ _ _ _ _ lifts a Graveler like a weight to make its muscles stronger. No matter how much it exercises, it never gets sore.

5. As a _ _ _ _ _ _ _ grows older, its rough edges are smoothed away. When it sleeps, it digs into the ground, where it resembles a rock.

6. Because its brain never stops growing, _ _ _ _ _ _ _ _ must use telekinesis to hold up its heavy head. On the plus side, its memory and intellect are amazing.

8. _ _ _ _ _ _ wraps its tail around solid objects on the seafloor to avoid being swept away in a strong current. When threatened, it spits a cloud of ink to cover its escape.

ACROSS

2. _ _ _ _ _ _ flies into a rage at the slightest provocation. These fits of temper are usually preceded by violent tremors, but there's rarely enough time to get away.

3. Though _ _ _ _ _ _ _ can use mysterious psychic powers, it can never remember doing so. Apparently, this power creates strange brain waves that resemble deep slumber.

4. The gases that fill the body of _ _ _ _ _ _ _ are extremely toxic. When it's under attack, it releases this poisonous gas from jets on its surface.

7. The red pouches on this Pokémon's cheeks store up electricity while it sleeps. It often delivers a zap when encountering something unfamiliar.

9. When this Pokémon's shell is closed, its large tongue tends to hang out. It uses its tongue as a shovel to dig a nest in the sand.

ANSWER ON PAGE 104

AN ALL RIGHT HEIGHT

Oh no! Clefable is stuck on a cliff, 36 feet off of the ground! Which Pokémon team can you use to get to Clefable? Remember, the Pokémon team you use have to reach Clefable at around 37 feet—36 feet won't reach it, and 38 feet will pass it up! You can only use each Pokémon once!

TEAM 1

21'04"

5'07"

1'08"

TEAM 2

1'00"

7'03"

28'10"

TEAM 3

6'07"

13'01"

3'03"

ANSWER ON PAGE 104

KANTO

JOHTO

HOENN

SINNOH

UNOVA

KALOS

WEIGHT FOR IT

Snorlax is asleep on the see-saw, and the other Pokémon want to play. Unfortunately, the only way to wake Snorlax up is to raise it off the ground—at least level with the other Pokémon! What is the fewest number of the following Pokémon that you can place on the left side of the see-saw to bring Snorlax level with the others? Remember, you want to get as close to Snorlax's weight as possible.

661.4 lbs.   70.5 lbs.   19.0 lbs.   264.6 lbs.

6.4 lbs.   14.3 lbs.   264.6 lbs.   11.9 lbs.

7.1 lbs.   143.3 lbs.

1,014.1 lbs.

KANTO

JOHTO

HOENN

SINNOH

UNOVA

KALOS

WHO'S THAT POKÉMON?

OK, regional specialist. You're doing well so far. But part of understanding your region specific Pokémon is the ability to guess what they are on sight. Can you guess which Pokémon these are based on their shadowy silhouettes?

1

2

3

4

5

6

BEEDRILL

RATTATA

RAICHU

VULPIX

PARAS

DUGTRIO

KANTO

JOHTO

HOENN

SINNOH

UNOVA

KALOS

PARTS NOT INCLUDED

It's a mixed up world out there in Kanto. Can you identify these Pokémon and their missing parts? Match the Kanto Pokémon to its appendages, and show everyone how a real regional specialist does it!

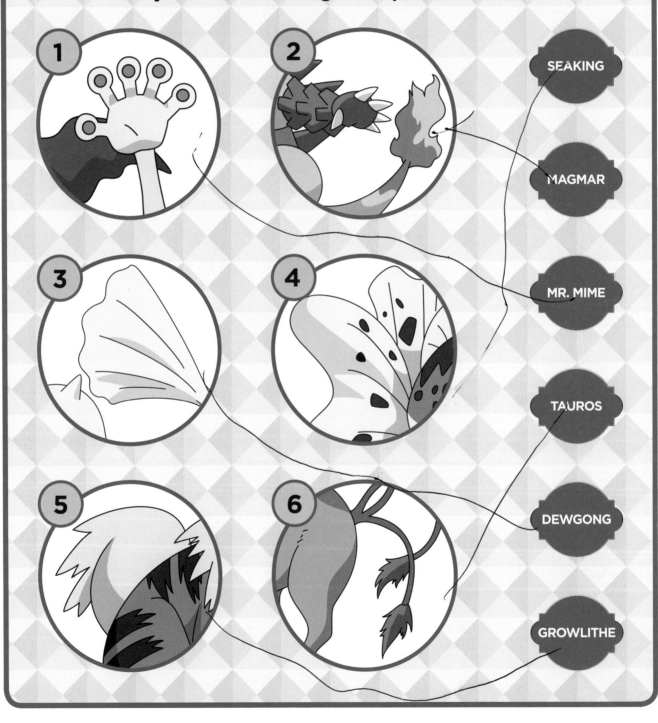

1

2

SEAKING

MAGMAR

3

4

MR. MIME

TAUROS

5

6

DEWGONG

GROWLITHE

ANSWER ON PAGE 104

SPOT THE DIFFERENCE

Not every Pokémon in Kanto is what it seems—
only an expert in regional Pokémon can tell the
subtle differences between Pokémon. See if you
can spot the real Pokémon—look for changes in
color, appendages, or even facial expressions.

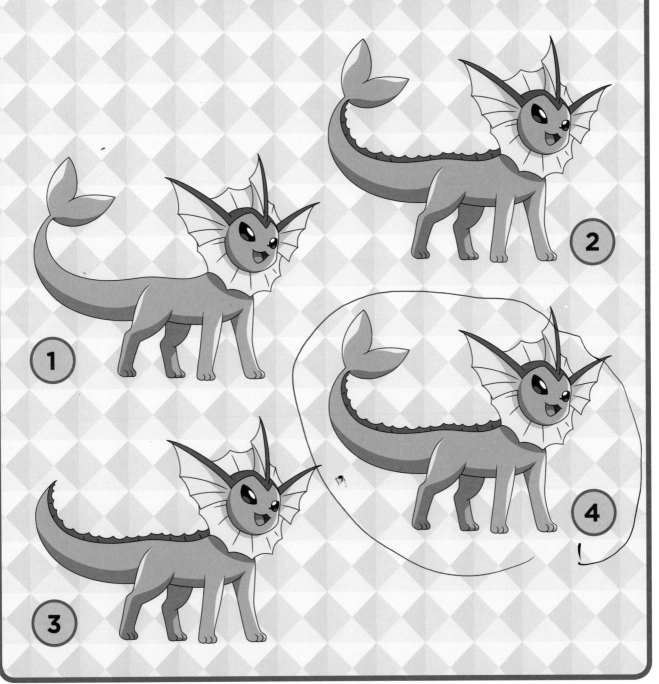

KANTO

JOHTO

HOENN

SINNOH

UNOVA

KALOS

KANTO

JOHTO

HOENN

SINNOH

UNOVA

KALOS

PUZZLER

Time to do a little investigative work. Using the key on page 101, decipher this code found on a Pokémon adventurer, and see what Pokémon they were trying to track down before they mysteriously disappeared!

This  Pokémon

often brings  in its

wake. When  flaps

its wings, the  turns chilly.

ANSWER ON PAGE 104

MAZE ME

Kanto mazes can be tricky—help Dratini find Dragonair, and then lead them both to Dragonite!

FINISH

START

KANTO

JOHTO

HOENN

SINNOH

UNOVA

KALOS

KANTO

JOHTO

HOENN

SINNOH

UNOVA

KALOS

FINISH THE POKÉMON

OK, regional specialist, let's see how well you know your Kanto Pokémon by sight. Can you finish sketching out this Kanto Pokémon from memory? 100 points if you don't peek at the Pokédex!

ANSWER ON PAGE 104

KANTO

JOHTO

HOENN

SINNOH

UNOVA

KALOS

END OF THE LINE

We're almost done in Kanto, and what better way to wrap things up than to identify the fully evolved first partner Pokémon. Can you spot Charizard, Blastoise, and Venusaur among the following Pokémon?

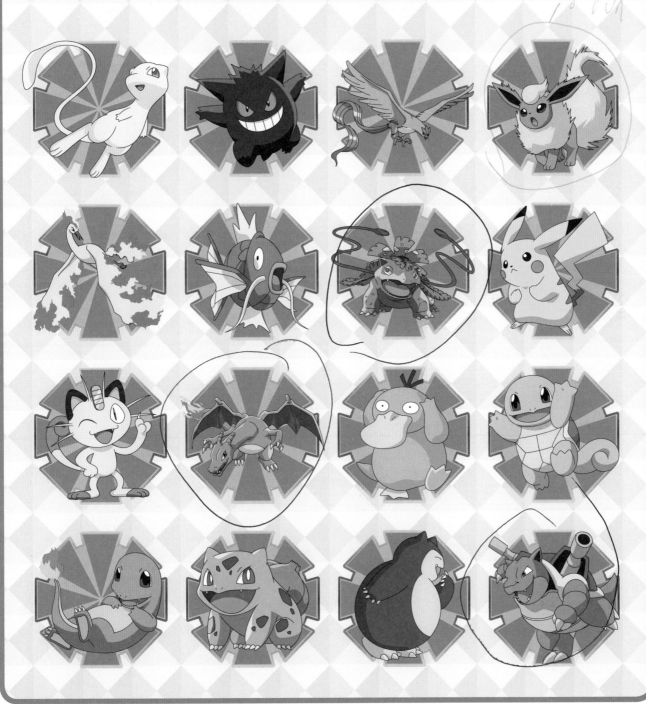

KANTO

JOHTO

HOENN

SINNOH

UNOVA

KALOS

Certificate of Completion

This is to certify that

Brxce

has achieved the rank of
Pokémon regional specialist
for the region of Kanto.

BULBASAUR

CHARMANDER

SQUIRTLE

IVYSAUR

CHARMELEON

WARTORTLE

VENUSAUR

CHARIZARD

BLASTOISE

Issued this ___March___ day of ___27___, 20 _16_

WELCOME TO THE JOHTO REGION

Welcome to Johto, Pokémon regional specialist. The next lineup of Pokémon includes some of the most fascinating ever seen. Let's see how well you know the Pokémon from the Johto region.

KANTO

JOHTO

HOENN

SINNOH

UNOVA

KALOS

KANTO

JOHTO

HOENN

SINNOH

UNOVA

KALOS

⊙ FIRST PARTNER POKÉMON ⊙

Let's start at the start! Can you identify
these first partner Pokémon from just
their silhouettes? One of these three will
start your journey through Johto!

1

2

3

KANTO
JOHTO
HOENN
SINNOH
UNOVA
KALOS

POKÉMON POETRY SLAM

Here are some clues about your favorite Johto Pokémon, left behind by a poetry lover that vacated the region recently and left behind a poetry journal. Can you identify which Johto Pokémon are the subjects of these poems?

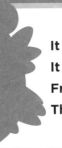

It knows how to sense sadness with its fluffy coat of fur,
It will rush to the aid of the lonely in a quick and steady blur,
Friend of a joyful nurse that's always super busy,
This Pokémon goes by the name of _____

It gets stressed when it isn't allowed to train,
You have to know its schedule, in sunshine or rain,
And although its style isn't always in vogue,
No one can deny the power of _Tyrgue_

It conceals itself quietly among the rocks,
Its tough shell prevents the hardiest knocks,
When captured in the wild it will rarely buckle,
It turns berries to juice and its name is _Shvale_

KANTO

JOHTO

HOENN

SINNOH

UNOVA

KALOS

⊙ WHO'S THAT POKÉMON? ⊙

Again, quickly identifying Pokémon, even when they zip in and out of the shadows, can be tricky business. See if you can identify these Johto Pokémon by their shadowy shapes.

1

2

4

3

5

6

7

LEDYBA

FLAAFFY

CROBAT

CHINCHOU

URSARING

MANTINE

STANTLER

◉ EVOLUTION REVOLUTION ◉

You know your first partner Pokémon, but do you know their Evolutions? See if you can guess the correct order and fill in the numbers and names below.

Chikorita → (3)_____ → (2)_____

Cyndaquil → (4)_____ → (1)_____

Totodile → (6)_____ → (5)_____

KANTO

JOHTO

HOENN

SINNOH

UNOVA

KALOS

◉ IT TAKES ALL TYPES ◉

Match the correct Johto Pokémon on the left to their type on the right. Remember, not every Pokémon looks like its type, and some of these have more than one type.

1

2

3

4

5

6

FAIRY

ROCK

NORMAL

DARK
FIRE

PSYCHIC

ELECTRIC

ANSWER ON PAGE 105

FINISH THE POKÉMON

How's your memory, regional specialist?
Let's see if you can finish this Pokémon from
memory! That'll show 'em who's boss!

KANTO

JOHTO

HOENN

SINNOH

UNOVA

KALOS

PUZZLER

Another expert has vanished in Johto—
but they left behind this cryptic clue
describing a Pokémon. See if you can decipher
which Pokémon this is using page 101!

Legend says their  __ __ __ __ __ __ __ __

bring joy to whoever holds one.

When  __ __ __ — __ __ 's feathers

catch the light at different angles,

they glow in a __ __ __ __ __ __ __ of colors.

28 ANSWER ON PAGE 105

KANTO

JOHTO

HOENN

SINNOH

UNOVA

KALOS

PARTS NOT INCLUDED

Another test of your Pokémon sighting abilities.
Each region has specific Pokémon—can you guess
what appendages belong to each?

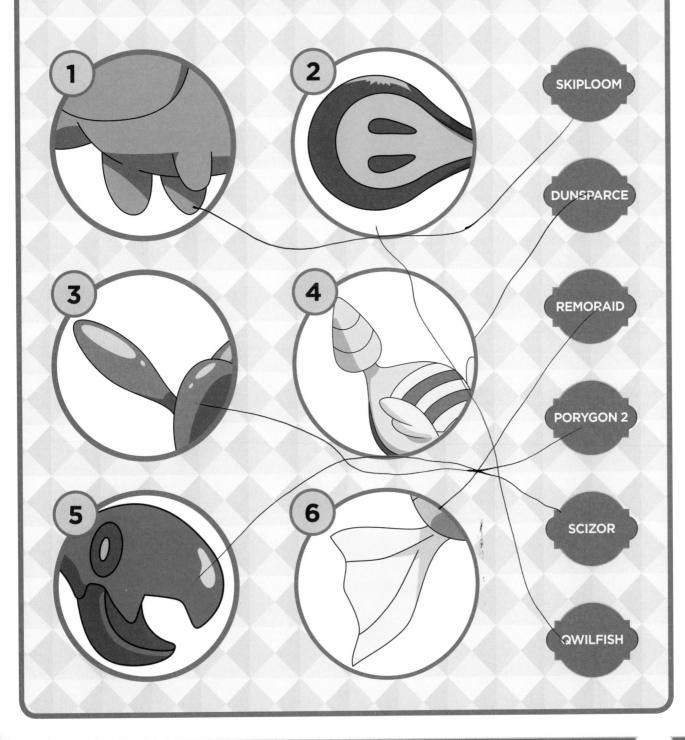

1

2

3

4

5

6

SKIPLOOM

DUNSPARCE

REMORAID

PORYGON 2

SCIZOR

QWILFISH

JOHTO WORD SEARCH

Let's double check your regional skills by having you identify only the 100 Johto Pokémon in this word search— be careful, though; a few non-Johto Pokémon are hidden in here as well!

```
F O R R E T R E S S J U M B R E O N R H A G T P K O B M P T
E Q H O M D N O C T O W L S H D E N D F O D O C W U A E S Y
R M A N K E Y L E D Y B A C F L A A F F Y T U Y E V Y G Y P
A T E X A T U L A N T U R N N H A E U R N D O W G E L A D H
L Y M O L M U R K R O W U N P I L O E O L E D I A N E N U L
I R A Z W R A I K O U L K N G C H P M O T O G E P I E I C O
G O R F S T A N T L E R O U S C O T G R A N B U L L F U K S
A G I A M B H A S P F D L F N O I A G D H O U N D O O M U I
T U L D U N S P A R C E E I W H O O T H O O T E A C S A R O
R E L C Y N D A Q U I L H E G E O K I N G D R A Y C K Y S N
V L H H B K I A A G K C V P L R N O P Q U I L A V A A D A F
V E H I Z P I N E C O Q E G I A Q T H E S P E O N O R Y R U
S K P K S U I C U N E A N B G C F D E G T E O G M I M D I R
P I E O M N Y H C O R S O L A R H L A I L A I X B P O W N R
I D R R O O S L O W K I N G R O E U S I M R 2 I R Y R S G E
N P S I O W A I A B G A A P I S Q O D G A N L A R W Y T C T
A O I T C N M B U N R X T R A S R O U F O E T E W M H E R O
R L A A H O U N D O U R U E Y A T L A G D I L E O S S E O G
A I N E U Z I I L J P S N C H O S R Y I V L N S I M N L B E
K T F Z M W A F M I U S C P T K I R L R I S S F N I U I A T
S O M R S R N O P B W M M I L G O L A T O O L R W L B X T I
C E A O O U P P W H O A P O Z P F L C D L I E S X T B B Y C
E D R M S I O O T D M G Z L I O Q O A L W K O E E A U L R R
L W E I A H G O O T D B M U U S R I E Q N L S V B N L I A O
E R E M D R M O T F G Y M K M F R B R U I V E X G K L S N C
B E P W A O W E M A N T I N E A F L S P A R A S E C T S I O
I K L C N O L U J J K T S M E A R G L E W O B B U F F E T N
R C G E D G D U G T R I O T E D D I U R S A P H A N P Y A A
I A V U I G G L Y B U F F Y A N M A L P U P I T A R K R R W
M I S D R E A V U S C S E N T R E T W L S K I P L O O M Z Z
```

JOHTO CROSSWORD

Being a regional specialist means knowing your Pokémon's information—from top to bottom. See if you can handle this crossword, which uses Pokédex descriptions for its clues.

8. C e l e b i

DOWN

1. It curls up in a ball to attack with a high-speed rolling tackle. Such an attack can knock down a house!

3. The brain that controls this Pokémon's secondary head is too small to think and just reacts to its surroundings. It tends to attack anyone who approaches from behind.

4. When this Pokémon roars, the air and land shudder. This Legendary Pokémon moves with lightning speed.

6. It can clear pollution from lakes and rivers. This Legendary Pokémon's heart is as pure as clear water.

9. It can knock down a house with one flutter of its enormously powerful wings. For the safety of others, this Legendary Pokémon lives at the bottom of the sea.

ACROSS

2. The steel that makes up _ _ _ _ _ _ _'s wings gets dinged up and dented during battles. Every year, the sharp edges renew themselves.

5. Though its feet end in sharp claws, _ _ _ _ _ _ _ _ _ doesn't use them as a weapon. Instead, it digs them into the ground to brace itself while it uses its giant horn to scoop up an enemy.

7. These can be found in many different shapes that resemble ancient writing. It's not known which came first.

8. _ _ _ _ _ _ traveled back in time to come to this world. According to myth, its presence is a sign of a bright future.

10. People say that _ _ _ _ _ came into being when a volcano erupted. This Legendary Pokémon carries the heat of magma in its fiery heart.

ANSWER ON PAGE 105

KANTO
JOHTO
HOENN
SINNOH
UNOVA
KALOS

POKÉMON ACROSTICS

Let's see how much you know about mixing up the Johto Pokémon names. Play this game with one, two, or three players.

RULES Pick a Pokémon name. Write that name in a column. If you pick a Pokémon like Sudowoodo, you should have a puzzle that looks like this. Now, spell the longest word you can with the letters in each row. For example, starting with the first letter, try to spell the longest word you can with "s", like "sentimentalist". You can only make one word per row, but you get a point for each letter in the word.

S _____

U _____

D _____

O _____

W _____

O _____

O _____

D _____

O _____

BONUS Time the game and see how many words you can make in two minutes. Give yourself an extra five points per line for spelling Pokémon names!

SPOT THE DIFFERENCE

See if you can spot the real Pokémon—look for changes in color, appendages, or facial expressions. Some Pokémon have minor differences that only a regional specialist could identify. Good luck!

1

2

3

4

KANTO

JOHTO

HOENN

SINNOH

UNOVA

KALOS

KANTO

JOHTO

HOENN

SINNOH

UNOVA

KALOS

⊙ MAZE ME ⊙

Help Houndour find its pack by linking it up with Houndoom. Be careful—this maze is a little tougher than the last one.

START

FINISH

ANSWER ON PAGE 105

END OF THE LINE

We've come to the end of the Johto region—you're almost certified as a regional specialist! Let's see if you can recognize the last Evolutions of Cyndaquil, Totodile, and Chikorita among these other Pokémon from Johto.

ANSWER ON PAGE 105

KANTO
JOHTO
HOENN
SINNOH
UNOVA
KALOS

Certificate of Completion

This is to certify that

_____

has achieved the rank of Pokémon regional specialist for the region of Johto.

CYNDAQUIL

TOTODILE

CHIKORITA

QUILAVA

CROCONAW

BAYLEEF

TYPHLOSION

FERALIGATR

MEGANIUM

Issued this _____ day of _____, 20 __

⊙ WELCOME TO ⊙ THE HOENN REGION

You are almost halfway through all of the Pokémon regions so far! Congratulations—but don't rest up just yet. Let's see what you know about the Pokémon of the Hoenn region!

KANTO

JOHTO

HOENN

SINNOH

UNOVA

KALOS

KANTO
JOHTO
HOENN
SINNOH
UNOVA
KALOS

⊙ FIRST PARTNER POKÉMON ⊙

Let's start with the first Pokémon you meet in Hoenn. Do you recognize these Pokémon by their silhouettes?

ANSWER ON PAGE 106

IT TAKES ALL TYPES

Knowing your Pokémon means knowing their types. Match these Hoenn Pokémon to their correct types, and be careful—some of them are dual types!

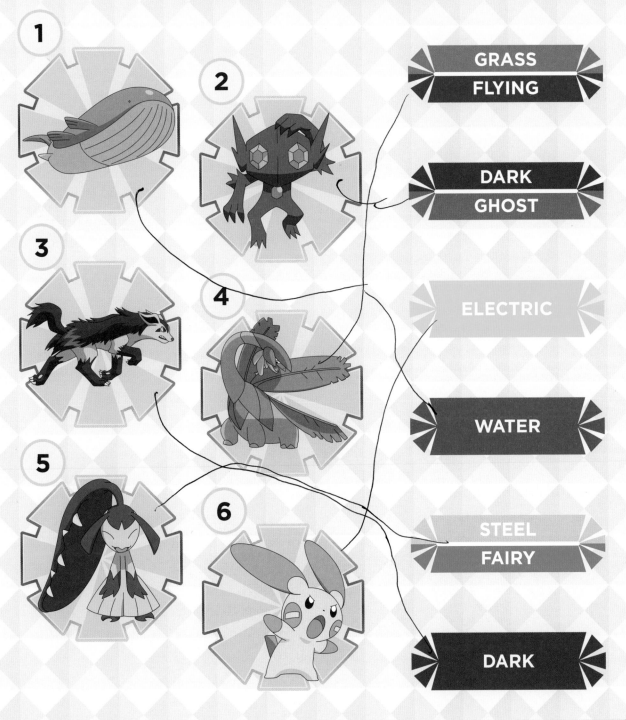

1

2

3

4

5

6

GRASS
FLYING

DARK
GHOST

ELECTRIC

WATER

STEEL
FAIRY

DARK

ANSWER ON PAGE 106

KANTO
JOHTO
HOENN
SINNOH
UNOVA
KALOS

SPOT THE DIFFERENCE

Don't be too hasty when spotting regional Pokémon. Although Pokémon look different, some have very specific markings—you have to look for appendages that are missing, colors that are different, or parts that are missing. Look at this Pokémon and pick out the one that is real, and circle the differences on the others.

1

2

3

4

ANSWER ON PAGE 106

KANTO

JOHTO

HOENN

SINNOH

UNOVA

KALOS

⊙━ EVOLUTION REVOLUTION ━⊙

You know your first partner Pokémon, but do you know their Evolutions? See if you can guess the correct order and fill in the numbers and names below.

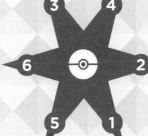

Treecko → (4)_____ → (6)_____
Torchic → (1)_____ → (2)_____
Mudkip → (3)_____ → (5)_____

KANTO

JOHTO

HOENN

SINNOH

UNOVA

KALOS

DOTS WHAT I'M TALKING ABOUT

There's a chance that a Pokémon is buzzing around sand dunes in Hoenn. Find out who this Pokémon is by investigating these clues!

CLUE 2:
It stirs up sand and creates a sandstorm

CLUE 1:
It evolves from Trapinch— eventually

CLUE 3:
It also produces musical tones with its wings

If you guessed it in:
One clue—Your expertise is exemplary
Two clues—Your Pokédex is filling up nicely
Three clues—You're on your way to becoming a regional specialist!

KANTO

JOHTO

HOENN

SINNOH

UNOVA

KALOS

POKÉMON NAME GAME

Hoenn experts know that a key to being the best is intelligence and quick wits. Here's a one-player, two-player, or multiplayer word game that tests how quickly you can identify Pokémon.

CHIMECHO

chime

him

ice

mice

echo

come

home

ohm

RULES

You and a friend pick out a Hoenn Pokémon, like Chimecho. Each of you then writes that Pokémon name down on a piece of paper. Now come up with as many words as you can using that Pokémon's letters within a two minute time limit. The player with the most words after two minutes wins.

KANTO

JOHTO

HOENN

SINNOH

UNOVA

KALOS

MATCH THE MOVE

Do you know your Hoenn Pokémon by name yet? Okay, then let's start with their Moves. Match the Hoenn Pokémon to its Move and see how much you know!

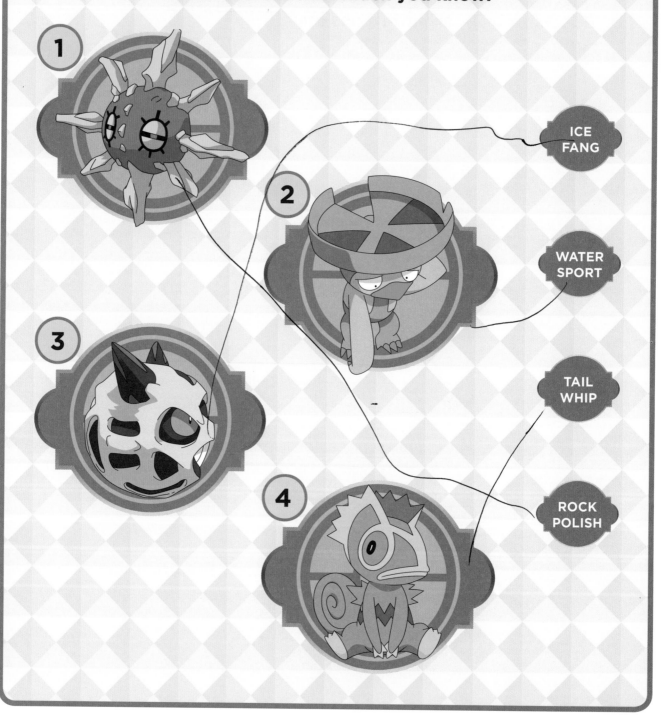

1

2

3

4

ICE FANG

WATER SPORT

TAIL WHIP

ROCK POLISH

ANSWER ON PAGE 106

HOENN WORD SEARCH

Now's your chance to prove you know your Hoenn Pokémon by name! Find the 135 Hoenn Pokémon in this word search, but be careful—a couple of Pokémon from other regions may appear in the word search as well.

```
D R M X S U R S K I T W V X H H U N T A I L Z Q B L X N B S H S L N B
U S A S H A R P E D O P L U D I C O L O N G H I B E I T A M S L O S A
S W W L T O R C H I C L A T I O S C O C A C N E A P U B A O U D L L N
K A I N T T R A P I N C H F G D S L A K I N G E L A E H R G U B O A E
U L L B N S S N O R U N T Q W W L A T I A S V U N E C G N O N L M K T
L O E Q G N V F M M A K U H I T A M W T Y H G Y F I A I R Y G A B O T
L T S A B L E Y E D U S C L O P S P U A C R W V D T W G P Y L Z R T E
L H F K I N G D R A W A I L M E R E R I L O Y E E L R N L A A I E H W
O M Z Z I G Z A G O O N F O C T E R M L A O M M B J A I O E L K W C C
U I B J G J W G F L C Y U R X A W L P L Y M H U K H D K T A I E C U V
D L A B U V H A L O J O G L E G C O L O D I A P P A R I P L E N A C V
R O R E S O I Z Y M H B R O H L R T E W O S R P R O T G B T X I R O H
E T B L W L S U G Y O J H P E O I U U I L H I C T I T M J A A N V M E
D I O D A B C R O L N C I G H T U C M R J X Y P D E R A K R R C A B L
U C A U M E A I N O E O Y R R I C N A P N S A E E W E N S I M A N U E
L H C M P A S L E M C L N P A O S W D N I E M E D E E E I A A D H S C
A G H Y E T H L I S F O S I B C V H A O T G A S C X C C L R L A A K T
I Q B P R J C H I I O U B A F A H Y F L O H F H R P K T C P D Z I E R
R I V O T A C D T C I S P H E A L I L U R M L E A L O R O F O X E N I
O L I O K S V U S P T D E L C A T T Y E O E C D W O T I O S P O I N K
N L G C J U A A O D O N P H A N L L O O M I I I D U S C N K N R S G E
R U O H L E C R S W E L L O W O B R L Y G G D N A D H J S U W Y W L S
W M R Y B V T N O S E P A S S P R E A E T D T J U T E C F E X R G U A
H I O E U S C Z F O P R L B O I R I R Y I C N A N W L C W O A H Z N L
I S T N X X Y A R M A E A M O B L C K S Q O C S T S G F E B T L G A A
S E H A O A E E S I E M Z V U E C A M E R U P T K M O D X I P Q E T M
M S D T D L R N L T A T E A S D N W M A S Y A V F A N R R C L S G O E
U H S N Z G O R S V F D A O N O K A T I S O D Z T U R O X R U H O N N
R U I U O G I I A C R O R N R G L I A V N Q L Q A S N M S E S I R E C
D P N Y A K G R N A Z R R G G C O L P B D U U R L A E S O Y L F E S E
S P K B K E B D G J C F G M M J T O V I D A N E O I P V K R E T B W M
V E K E R I M N I N J A S K T M A R S H T O M P R C L X I I Y R Y A G
S T G J V S C E P T I L E Z O C D D R E N I Q M E A K E C P T Y S B T
P E L I P P E R N U M E L O M I G H T Y E N A A U Y I Y E O E T S L L
D J L I N O O N E Z U S E E D O T P R E G I R O C K S N B P R R Y U F
```

KANTO

JOHTO

HOENN

SINNOH

UNOVA

KALOS

PUZZLER

Another cryptic clue, and another Pokémon in the Hoenn region that you might spot! This diary entry was found, and using the key on page 101 you can decipher what Pokémon this adventurer spotted before it disappeared!

Dear Diary,

Minerals from the  _ _ _ _ _

become part of its gemstone  _ _ _ _

and the  _ _ _ _ _ _ _ _ on its body.

 _ _ _ _ _ _ _ lives deep in

a  _ _ _ _ where it uses its

sharp  _ _ _ _ _ to dig up rocks

for  _ _ _ _ .

ANSWER ON PAGE 106

KANTO

JOHTO

HOENN

SINNOH

UNOVA

KALOS

HOENN CROSSWORD

You are so boss at being a Pokémon expert! You definitely have your Hoenn Pokémon down—but let's see if you can solve this crossword with its mix of Mythical and Legendary Pokémon!

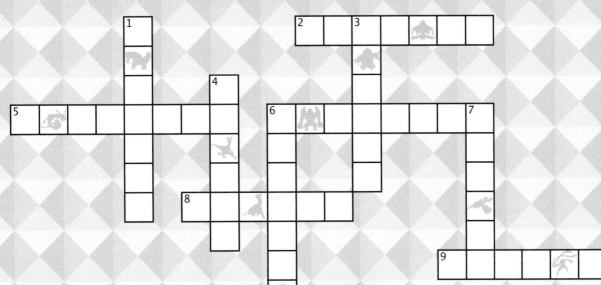

DOWN

1. Legends say that _ _ _ _ _ _ _ is the land personified. When it channels the full power of nature, it can expand the land-mass with eruptions of magma. This Pokémon often clashes with Kyogre.

3. Created during an ice age, its body is frozen solid, and even lava can't melt it. It can lower the temperature of the air around it by several hundred degrees.

4. Sensitive and intelligent, this Pokémon can pick up on people's emotions and understand what they're saying. The down that covers its body can refract light to change its appearance.

6. It isn't actually made of steel—it's a strange substance harder than any known metal. Ancient people sealed it away in a prison.

7. Legends say that _ _ _ _ _ _ _ is the sea personified. When it channels the full power of nature, it can raise sea levels with mighty storms. This Pokémon often clashes with Groudon.

ACROSS

2. According to myth, if you write your wish on one of the notes attached to its head and then sing to it in a pure voice, the Pokémon will awaken from its thousand-year slumber and grant your wish.

5. Legends say this ancient Pokémon flies through the upper atmosphere and feeds on meteoroids. It's known for stopping the endless battles between Kyogre and Groudon.

6. Its body is made entirely of rocks, and these rocks were recently discovered to be from all around the world. It repairs itself after battle by seeking out new rocks.

8. _ _ _ _ _ _ can project images into someone else's mind to share information. When it folds its forelegs back against its body, it could beat a jet plane in a race through the sky.

9. From the crystal on its chest, _ _ _ _ _ _ can shoot out laser beams. This highly intelligent Pokémon came into being when a virus mutated during a fall from space.

KANTO
JOHTO
HOENN
SINNOH
UNOVA
KALOS

WALL SCRAWL

Clues everywhere! Someone has tried to tell us about some of the Hoenn Pokémon, but they only wrote their names phonetically on the inside of a cave. Can you turn this gibberish into sense?

1 KNOWS PAS

2 LOO NAT OWN

5 MASK AH RAIN

3 VIG ER ROTH

4 SAL UH MENCE

6 KAI OG UHR

7 HAR EE YAH MAH

9 WHY NOT

8 SEEL EE OH

10 CORE FISH

MAZE ME

Help Castform go through the maze and watch it change Forms with the weather. Its mood changes with the weather too!

START

FINISH

KANTO

JOHTO

HOENN

SINNOH

UNOVA

KALOS

KANTO

JOHTO

HOENN

SINNOH

UNOVA

KALOS

WHO'S THAT POKÉMON?

Ready for something a little more intense? See if you can quickly identify these Pokémon by just their shadows. A regional specialist should be able to quickly and correctly identify a Pokémon—even if they only have a few seconds to do so. Go to it and good luck!

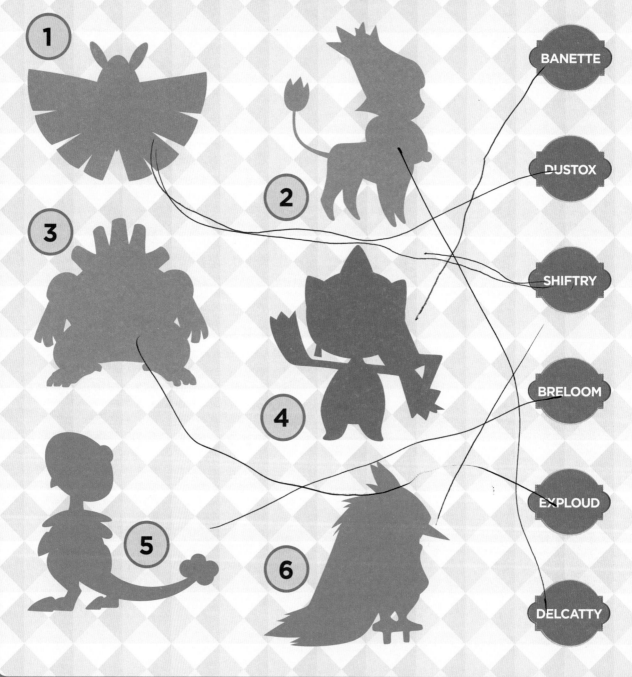

1

2

3

4

5

6

BANETTE

DUSTOX

SHIFTRY

BRELOOM

EXPLOUD

DELCATTY

ANSWER ON PAGE 107

END OF THE LINE

You did it! You made it through Hoenn with flying colors. Now, as a final test, see if you can find the final Evolutions of Mudkip, Treecko, and Torchic amidst these other Hoenn Pokémon!

KANTO

JOHTO

HOENN

SINNOH

UNOVA

KALOS

ANSWER ON PAGE 107

KANTO

JOHTO

HOENN

SINNOH

UNOVA

KALOS

Certificate of Completion

This is to certify that

_____

has achieved the rank of
Pokémon regional specialist
for the region of Hoenn.

TREECKO

MUDKIP

TORCHIC

GROVYLE

MARSHTOMP

COMBUSKEN

SCEPTILE

SWAMPERT

BLAZIKEN

Issued this _____ day of _____, 20 __

⦿ WELCOME TO ⦿ THE SINNOH REGION

More Pokémon abound in Sinnoh, with the impressive Mt. Coronet dividing the region. You're going to see a lot of differences on the two opposing sides of the mountain, so let's begin with the identification of Pokémon!

KANTO

JOHTO

HOENN

SINNOH

UNOVA

KALOS

KANTO

JOHTO

HOENN

SINNOH

UNOVA

KALOS

⊙ FIRST PARTNER POKÉMON ⊙

Let's start at the start! Can you identify these first partner Pokémon from just their silhouettes? These are the three that will start your journey through Sinnoh!

KANTO

JOHTO

HOENN

SINNOH

UNOVA

KALOS

WHO'S THAT POKÉMON?

Ready for something a little more intense? See if you can quickly identify these Pokémon by just their shadows. A regional specialist should be able to quickly and correctly identify a Pokémon—even if they only have a few seconds to do so. Go to it and good luck!

1

2

3

4

5

6

VESPIQUEN

CHATOT

BUIZEL

PACHIRISU

CROAGUNK

MAGNEZONE

ANSWER ON PAGE 107

KANTO

JOHTO

HOENN

SINNOH

UNOVA

KALOS

POKÉMON NAME GAME

A Sinnoh regional specialist should have a little fun when identifying new Pokémon. Let's take a break and play a Pokémon name game that will test your skill and intelligence level.

ABOMASNOW

bow

boa

snow

man

now

ban

bow

nab

RULES

You and a friend pick out a Sinnoh Pokémon, like Abomasnow. Each of you then writes that Pokémon name down on a piece of paper. Now come up with as many words as you can using that Pokémon's letters within a two minute time limit. The player with the most words after two minutes wins.

EVOLUTION REVOLUTION

You know your first partner Pokémon, but do you know their Evolutions? See if you can guess the correct order and fill in the numbers and names below.

Turtwig → (3)_____ → (2)_____
Chimchar → 6)_____ → (1)_____
Piplup → (4)_____ → (5)_____

KANTO

JOHTO

HOENN

SINNOH

UNOVA

KALOS

⊙ SINNOH WORD SCRAMBLE ⊙

To train Pokémon, you need to know everything about them. Help us identify which Pokémon this is by unscrambling the letters hidden in the clues below. Fill in the puzzle, then use the highlighted letters to find the Pokémon!

- It's a Water- and ☐ round-type Pokémon
  1

- It evolves from a Shell ☐ s
  2

- It is the Sea ☐ lug Pokémon
  3

- They were once covered by protective shells, but over the ☐ ges, those shells have vanished.
  4

- When ☐ hreatened, they release pu ☐ ple fluid to cover their escape.
  5   6

- It uses Mu ☐ dy Water as a move
  7

- It also has Body Slam in its arse ☐ al
  8

- It has 2 different appearances, depending where it is f ☐ und
  9

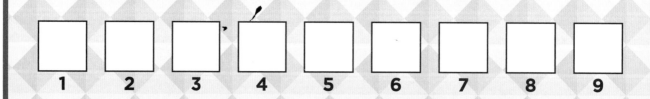

| 1 | 2 | 3 | 4 | 5 | 6 | 7 | 8 | 9 |

Unscramble to reveal the missing Pokémon.

IT TAKES ALL TYPES

You know your region, and you seem to know your Pokémon, so let's see if you know your Pokémon types. Match the Pokémon on the left with the types on the right. Be careful—some of the Pokémon are dual types.

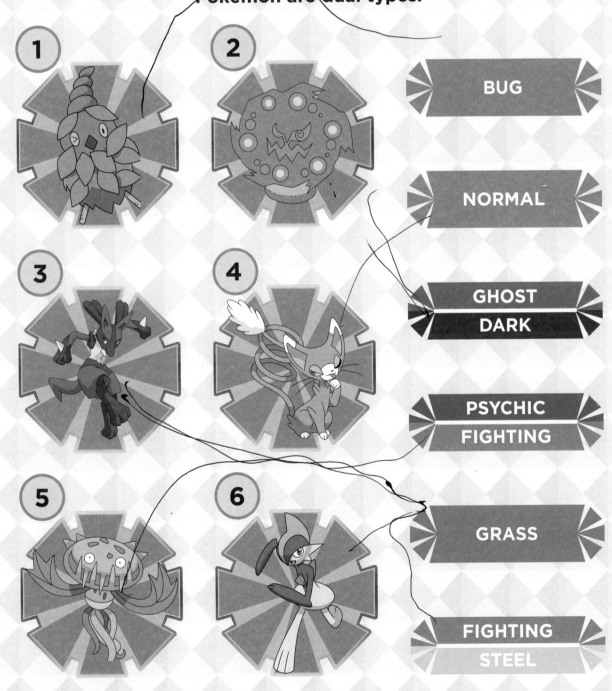

1

2

BUG

NORMAL

3

4

GHOST
DARK

PSYCHIC
FIGHTING

5

6

GRASS

FIGHTING
STEEL

KANTO
JOHTO
HOENN
SINNOH
UNOVA
KALOS

ANSWER ON PAGE 108 59

KANTO

JOHTO

HOENN

SINNOH

UNOVA

KALOS

WEIGHT FOR IT

Rhyperior is challenging the other Pokémon to lift it off the ground by sitting on the other side of the see-saw. What is the smallest number of the following Pokémon that you can place on the left side of the see-saw to bring Rhyperior level with the others? Remember, you want to get as close to Rhyperior's weight as possible.

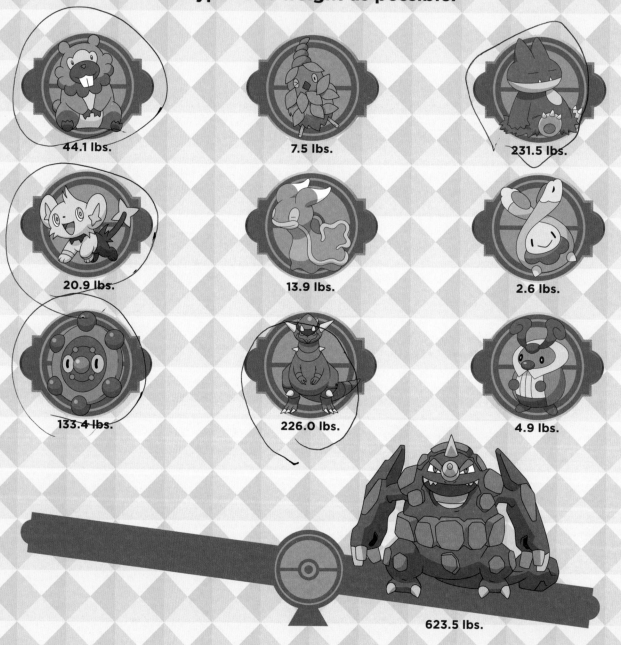

44.1 lbs.

7.5 lbs.

231.5 lbs.

20.9 lbs.

13.9 lbs.

2.6 lbs.

133.4 lbs.

226.0 lbs.

4.9 lbs.

623.5 lbs.

ANSWER ON PAGE 108

KANTO
JOHTO
HOENN
SINNOH
UNOVA
KALOS

SPOT THE DIFFERENCE

Sinnoh Pokémon can be tricky—like we said, you will see subtle differences between those on the East side of Mt. Coronet and those on the West side. But let's take a look at one Pokémon and see if you can identify the differences in their shapes. Spot the real Pokémon, and circle the difference in each.

1

2

3

4

KANTO

JOHTO

HOENN

SINNOH

UNOVA

KALOS

⊙ ODD POKÉMON OUT ⊙

So you know your Pokémon by sight—but can you sort out Pokémon that stand out in a crowd?

For this test, we're going to show you some different Sinnoh Pokémon. One of these doesn't belong in the group, but which one? And what is the group? We'll give you three clues—you score yourself by how many clues you used!

CLUE 1:
Once you guess correctly the grass will seem greener

Just 4 fun

CLUE 2:
All are one and one is two

CLUE 3:
Beware of Poison mixed with Grass

SCORING

One clue—You are a regional specialist
Two clues—You're doing well
Three clues—You will one day be in the regional specialists hall of fame.

ANSWER ON PAGE 108

KANTO

JOHTO

HOENN

SINNOH

UNOVA

KALOS

 # SINNOH WORD SEARCH

Okay, let's see if you can spot the Pokémon in the Sinnoh region by name. Below is a jumble of 107 Sinnoh Pokémon—some are spelled correctly, some may be backwards, and some may be diagonal. But wait—the list includes a few Pokémon that are not found in Sinnoh—don't be fooled and seek out the wrong ones! Find your Pokémon carefully.

```
L X U C H E R U B I P R O B O P A S S U N O S A B L E Y E H
I C X R G S D Y S T A R A V I A Z E L F I J R G R O T L E I
C P I E A K C H I M C H A R S N O V E R D I A L G A M S C P
K T E S L U P M O T H I M E D I C H A M I S M A G I U S U P
I U M S L N V E S P I Q U E N R B C J A Y M P M O Q N M H O
L R I E A T P Y I Y R C R O A G U N K M H A A B L P C O M P
I T M L D A K A G W I M A W I L E B F O B N R I U R H N E O
C W E I E N R N O X S J C R T U P E I S R T D P X I L F S T
K I J A U K A N N A U O O K N M L O N W O Y O O R N A E P A
Y G R T R R S I G N S N M L A I R O N I N K S M A P X R R S
J X S A T A H E O L O H B A V N V N E N Z E A R Y L P N I E
O H D A M S M D E D R X E A R E O I O E O R H R X U G O T J
H P E O U N O R O O X Y E L S O C F N R N N A Q L P W I S I
Y H B E A I A R Z M G W T A L N N O R E G E Z P G O B S P N
L A C Y T B T N A N P R G F O O I F G O N S I O R A I Z I F
E R K S I S O D I M A I I I G H S G L U S P T K G K M S R E
A A A B A R A L O T G R X J P R T I B O I S H A E P E T I R
F B B G B M G H R I D U S K N O I R F P A C L G R L R A T N
E E E R R N C O G G L M A G N E Z O N E N T O A B L H R O A
O M V O I R M E D I T I T E F P H L L O S T Z I S R Y A M P
N P W H A G R O S E R A D E C C Q O H U W O G E Q S P P B E
F O C G A P Y O N H G L I S C O R P I C P R L R L O E T N U
B L O M B H D U U D E L C A T T Y U P H A T A O M F R O D N
U E G C P I T A N G R O W T H W A N P E L E C T I V I R E S
D O V A N E B I D O O F B U R M Y N O R K R E O U P O R O H
E N N A K B U I Z E L P U R U G L Y W R I R O M A M R U R A
W A R C A G G R O N G I R A T I N A D I A A N R B O N S L Y
M C I T W S K O R U P I C H A T O T O M E Y D R I F B L I M
H R I G L A M E O W S H I E L D O N N A T O X I C R O A K I
K R I C K E T O T Z X F P O R Y G O N-Z Z H A P P I N Y V N
```

KANTO

JOHTO

HOENN

SINNOH

UNOVA

KALOS

PUZZLER

Another mysterious clue by an adventurer who has disappeared in Sinnoh! What Pokémon were they trying to find? Decipher this clue using page 101 to find out.

They take  _ _ _ _ _ _

at  _ _ _ _ ,

but since they can't control their direction,

they'll drift away

wherever the  _ _ _ _ blows them.

During the day,  _ _ _ _ _ _ _

tend to be  _ _ _ _ _ _ .

 ANSWER ON PAGE 108

MAZE ME

Gible needs to find its way to Garchomp, but first it needs to pick up Gabite. Help Gible find its way to the middle of the maze, and then out to the end!

FINISH

START

KANTO
JOHTO
HOENN
SINNOH
UNOVA
KALOS

SINNOH CROSSWORD

Sinnoh is filled with Legendary and Mythical Pokémon—and we've dedicated a crossword puzzle just to them!

DOWN

1. It is said this Legendary Pokémon can control time with its mighty roar. In ancient times, it was revered as a legend.

3. It is said it can cause rents and distortions in space. In ancient times, it was revered as a legend.

4. According to legend, _ _ _ _ _ _ _ _ _ built smaller models of itself out of rock, ice, and magma. It's so enormous that it could tow an entire continent behind it.

6. It defends its territory by sending intruders into a deep sleep, where they are tormented by terrible nightmares.

9. _ _ _ _ _ _ _ makes its home in caves carved out by volcanic eruptions. This Legendary Pokémon's feet can dig into rock, allowing it to walk on walls and ceilings.

10. In the mythology of the Sinnoh region, it emerged from its Egg into complete nothingness, and then shaped the world and everything in it.

ACROSS

2. According to legend, it brought the first taste of joy and sorrow to people's hearts. It is known as "The Being of Emotion."

5. _ _ _ _ _ _ gather in large groups as they drift with the current through warm seas. After floating for a time, they always return home, no matter how far they have traveled.

7. As punishment, this Legendary Pokémon was banished to another dimension, where everything is distorted and reversed.

8. From its earliest days, it possesses the power to form close bonds with any Pokémon, no matter what kind.

11. According to legend, it brought a lasting balance to the world. It is known as "The Being of Willpower."

12. When the Gracidea flower blooms, this Pokémon gains the power of flight. Wherever it goes, it clears the air of toxins and brings feelings of gratitude.

KANTO

JOHTO

HOENN

SINNOH

UNOVA

KALOS

END OF THE LINE

Wow. Amazing! You've done great so far, blasting through four regions and correctly identifying Pokémon from each region. One last test for Sinnoh—find the last Evolutions of the first partner Pokémon from page 54 among all of these Sinnoh Pokémon. Good luck!

KANTO

JOHTO

HOENN

SINNOH

UNOVA

KALOS

Certificate of Completion

This is to certify that

_____

has achieved the rank of
Pokémon regional specialist
for the region of Sinnoh.

PIPLUP

CHIMCHAR

TURTWIG

PRINPLUP

MONFERNO

GROTLE

EMPOLEON

INFERNAPE

TORTERRA

Issued this _____ day of _____, 20 ___

WELCOME TO THE UNOVA REGION

Wow, you really have gone through all the regions in style! You've identified Pokémon from Kanto, Johto, Hoenn, and Sinnoh. Now we enter the Unova region, with locales like the White Ruins, Mistralton Tower, and New Tork City. Let's see how you fare in Unova, regional specialist!

KANTO

JOHTO

HOENN

SINNOH

UNOVA

KALOS

KANTO
JOHTO
HOENN
SINNOH
UNOVA
KALOS

⊙ FIRST PARTNER POKÉMON ⊙

Let's begin at the beginning. Here are the first partner Pokémon you will meet in Unova. See if you can identify them just by their silhouette. Remember, regional specialists need to be quick on their feet, both mentally and physically!

ANSWER ON PAGE 109

KANTO
JOHTO
HOENN
SINNOH
UNOVA
KALOS

UNOVA CROSSWORD

Let's see if you can help figure out which Pokémon are being discussed below. Your Pokémon knowledge about Unova will shine if you can figure out this puzzle.

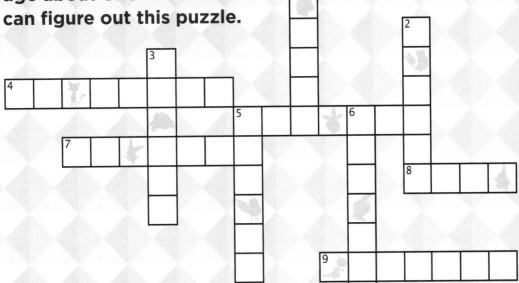

DOWN

1. When it attaches itself to something, it leaves a heart-shaped mark with its nose. The nose is also the source of its echolocation signals.

2. When it stretches out its limbs, the membrane connecting them spreads like a cape and allows it to glide through the air. It makes its abode high in the trees.

3. They can't produce their own electricity, so they attach to larger Pokémon and suck up the static electricity given off. They store this energy in a special pouch.

5. Even wild _ _ _ _ _ _ are used to having people around. They live in cities and often flock to places where people spend time, like plazas and parks.

6. It pretends to guide people and Pokémon with its light, but following it is a bad idea. The ghostly flame absorbs life energy for use as fuel.

ACROSS

4. It acts cute and innocent to trick people into trusting it. Then it steals their stuff.

5. When many of these settle in an area, gardeners and farmers pay attention, because these Pokémon seek out rich soil that's good for growing plants. Their leaves have healing properties.

7. According to myth, this Pokémon can bring victory in any kind of competition. Because it creates unlimited energy, it can share the overflow with others.

8. If one of this Pokémon's tusks breaks off, it quickly regrows, even stronger and sharper than before. It uses its tusks to crush berries and mark territory.

9. _ _ _ _ _ _ _ _ can pull its loose, rubbery skin up around its neck to protect itself from attacks. With its tough skull, it delivers headbutts without warning.

KANTO

JOHTO

HOENN

SINNOH

UNOVA

KALOS

⊙ WHO'S THAT POKÉMON? ⊙

Another sighting of Pokémon, but once again, they're quick! You're only going to get a glimpse of their shadows—see how many you can spot and correctly name.

SIGILYPH

YAMASK

TRUBBISH

MINCCINO

DEERLING

MUNNA

TYNAMO

1

2

3

4

5

6

7

EVOLUTION REVOLUTION

You know your first partner Pokémon, but do you know their Evolutions? See if you can guess the correct order and fill in the numbers and names below.

Snivy → (5)_____ → (6)_____
Tepig → (9)_____ → (4)_____
Oshawott → (3)_____ → (2)_____

KANTO

JOHTO

HOENN

SINNOH

UNOVA

KALOS

WORD SEARCH

See if you can identify all of the 156 Unova Pokémon in the word search, but be careful—there's a few non-Unova Pokémon mixed in there.

```
W H I R L I P E D E C K R O K O R O K D G E N E S E C T S D K Z H R K S
H E G B S S Z E B S T R I K A J U E X C A D R I L L N U R C S P R R A E
I L S L A B O M A S N O W L J T M C O N K E L D U R R A I U Y U U A M I
M G C B C R U S T L E F A R E S S A H Y A M A S K O P W R L B L G E C S
S Y R R C E M B O A R N O M L X P R N A J U R R X E T O I M O L Y R G M
I E A A E A U D I N O M L P L V A R O T N N O A I I D G I G O E R N R I
C M F V L A S X A G T E R N I I W A S D Y D H L L N I T O M E U A E A T
O M T I G C H U O A H A I A C C N C H E M K E J A S A N E H D L I U A O
T A Y A O U A Y E S H O G D E O I O A I A I E L G I I E E R K D R R E A
T R X R R B R H D S L U V N N T A S W N N V E J U C A B U N R O T D H D
P A U Y P C N K I R O M A H T T R T O O D M Q N C R Q G I E Z A L Y M A
I C N S E H A B R T E T S E H O D A T L I C P N S V E L H X P E K O E X
G T F W T O B U R L I I L D R N B W T A B D I C G H K R O O K O D I L E
N U E A I O P I L N L K G O O E E T D R U C D T Y N A M O O N G U S O W
I S Z N L Q T E A L C H D O H E A V E V Z R O R E S R O Z L C L M R E N
T N A N I E T M I U Q O U S N N R R W E Z P V D U O R M W A O A U S T S
E I N A L I R R D V B E E L E K T R O S S Q E L W S A C E P F M N I T O
P V T F H A F E R R O S E E D Q I C T T G P C Z E A B Z I S A P N M A L
I Y F T D R R E A T E N N L S G C K T A I I D E A W L O L R G E A I E O
G U O I R R D G R L H O F R E Z O E Y N N A W K V S A R O E R N V S M S
R G J D P U U U I R O U U R C K D L E U O T A R I B S O U S I T A E P I
N O A I W K B D O L O B N K A E T V E T R M Y O L U T A S H G N N A A S
Z T Z L W E N B D S L T S D P X I R I T U E T M E C B R R I U A I R N A
R H O A V A B A I I I U H I U M U P I R T M M F P K X K Q R S M L T P M
R O S U S A W B R S G O L O F R L R A K I A L O M O M O L A N I L L O U
J R E S S S N D L N H O N V R A U D E E R L I N G Z L T C M T N I I U R
T I R I T I N T O E C R N K P N H S U G I G A L I T H E B B A C T L R O
R T V M U M Q O U S T O U T L A N D U R D V O L C A R O N A T C E L M T
A A I I N I F Q A L U A R C H E O P S Z A A A H N B Z V I C T I N I S T
N J N S F P L E A V A N N Y M A G N E Z O N E N P A N S E A R N S G E O
Q O E A I O F C W A T C H O G M Z G O T H I T A I V I R I Z I O N A W R
U L P G S U S C R A G G Y M S W O O B A T L K U E L C O B A L I O N A N
I T M E K R O G G E N R O L A F B L I T Z L E L B O L D O R E R V T D A
L I L L I P U P E V A B O U F F A L A N T I C B A S C U L I N O E Q D D
L K B Q V S E R P E R I O R I W M R P A N S A G E N Z L X F O C R X L U
E S C A V A L I E R V V U L L A B Y A R C H E N V O G M I E N F O O E S
N U T R U B B I S H L K G O O E E Y D R U C D T Y N A M O O N G U S S W
```

KANTO

JOHTO

HOENN

SINNOH

UNOVA

KALOS

PUZZLER

Yikes! More regional specialists have fled the scene, but they left behind a hastily scrawled message on a crumpled piece of paper. Smooth it out and see if you can tell what Pokémon they were trailing! Use the key on page 101 for help.

 ___ ___ ___ ___ ___ ___ ___ tell of a time when this

Pokémon attacked a mighty  ___ ___ ___ ___ ___ ___

to protect its Pokémon friends.

 ___ ___ ___ ___ say it knocked down

a  ___ ___ ___ ___ ___ wall

with the ___ ___ ___ ___ ___ of its charge.

I saw a ___ ___ ___ ___ ___ ___ ___ ___ ___ !

KANTO

JOHTO

HOENN

SINNOH

UNOVA

KALOS

SPOT THE DIFFERENCE

There are many Pokémon in Unova, and not all of them look alike. Actually, some of them look just like real Pokémon, but they're impostors. See if you can spot the real Pokémon—look for changes in color, appendages, or facial expressions.

(1)

(2)

(3)

(4)

KANTO

JOHTO

HOENN

SINNOH

UNOVA

KALOS

MAZE ME

Seems like Legendary Pokémon are all over Unova. If you're trying to recognize all of the Pokémon in Unova, then you'll be psyched to know that Tornadus, Landorus, and Thundurus have been spotted, but you have to work this maze to find them.

START

FINISH

KANTO

JOHTO

HOENN

SINNOH

UNOVA

KALOS

PARTS UNKNOWN

Sometimes, you only get a glimpse of a Pokémon as it pops out of the grass or ocean or cave its hiding in. Match the Unova Pokémon to its appendages, and show everyone how a real regional specialist does it!

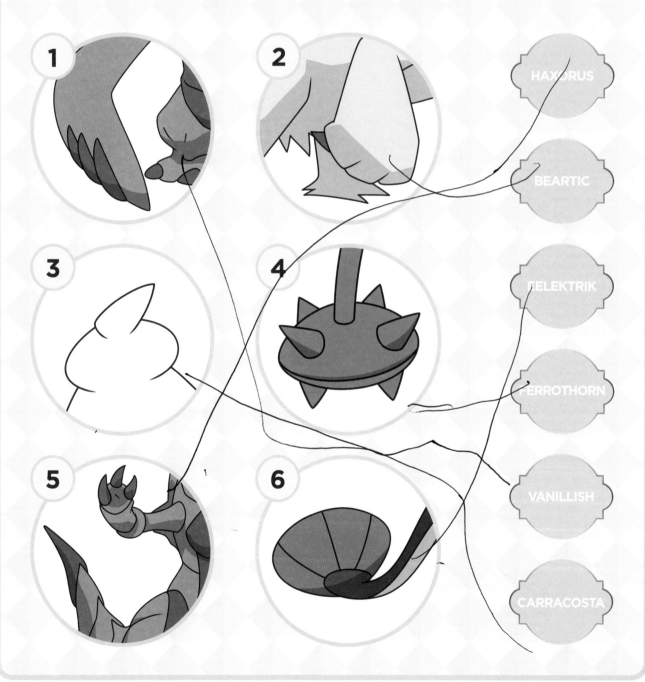

1

2

3

4

5

6

HAXORUS

BEARTIC

EELEKTRIK

FERROTHORN

VANILLISH

CARRACOSTA

KANTO

JOHTO

HOENN

SINNOH

UNOVA

KALOS

WEIGHT FOR IT

Uh oh! Golurk is balanced on the edge of a cliff. Thankfully, it's resting on a steel beam, and some of its Pokémon friends have rushed to the rescue. How few Pokémon can you put on the other side of the beam in order to balance Golurk out? Get as close to Golurk's weight as possible—too light and it will fall, too many and it will be launched into the air!

297.6 lbs.

0.7 lbs.

44.1 lbs.

181.9 lbs.

1.3 lbs.

154.3 lbs.

1.3 lbs.

27.6 lbs.

727.5 lbs.

33.1 lbs.

22.3 lbs.

KANTO

JOHTO

HOENN

SINNOH

UNOVA

KALOS

POKÉMON ACROSTICS

Let's see how much you know about mixing up the Unova Pokémon names. Play this game with one, two or three players.

RULES

Pick a Pokémon name. Write that name in a column. If you pick a Pokémon like Whirlipede, you should have a puzzle that looks like this. Now, spell the longest word you can with the letters in each row. For example, starting with the first letter, try to spell the longest word you can with "W", like "wholeheartedly." You can only make one word per row, but you get a point for each letter in the word.

W _____

H _____

I _____

R _____

L _____

I _____

P _____

E _____

D _____

E _____

BONUS Time the game and see how many words you can make in two minutes. Give yourself an extra five points per line for spelling Pokémon names!

KANTO

JOHTO

HOENN

SINNOH

UNOVA

KALOS

AN ALL RIGHT HEIGHT

A Zweilous is looking for something tasty to eat, but it can't reach the Berries stored on a high shelf in the training room. The shelf is 25 feet from the ground, but at 26 feet, the roof slopes in. Circle the fewest number of Pokémon that could get to the shelf if they climbed on top of one another to create a chain. Remember, they must be between 25 and 26 feet.

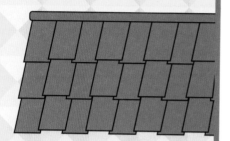

4'07"   3'07"   1'8"   4'07"

3'03"   1'00"   5'11"   5'03"

2'00"   1'04"   2'11"   5'03"

KANTO

JOHTO

HOENN

SINNOH

UNOVA

KALOS

FINISH THE POKÉMON

Great job so far—let's see if you can finish a Pokémon just using your memory. Here's half drawn Pokémon, Liepard. Finish this Pokémon to show us what your mind is made of.

HINT: Don't forget its spots!

ANSWER ON PAGE 110

END OF THE LINE

You should be proud—you passed all of Unova's many tests. Now all you need to do is find the last Evolutions of the first partner Pokémon on page 70 hidden among these other Unova Pokémon.

KANTO

JOHTO

HOENN

SINNOH

UNOVA

KALOS

ANSWER ON PAGE 110

KANTO

JOHTO

HOENN

SINNOH

UNOVA

KALOS

Certificate of Completion

This is to certify that

_____

has achieved the rank of Pokémon regional specialist for the region of Unova.

TEPIG

OSHAWATT

SNIVY

PIGNITE

DEWOTT

SERVINE

EMBOAR

SAMUROTT

SERPERIOR

Issued this _____ day of _____, 20 __

◉ WELCOME TO ◉ THE KALOS REGION

This is it—the latest explored region of Pokémon. In Kalos, you'll see so many new places and mysterious locales, with the Pokémon to match. Good luck!

KANTO

JOHTO

HOENN

SINNOH

UNOVA

KALOS

KANTO

JOHTO

HOENN

SINNOH

UNOVA

KALOS

◉ FIRST PARTNER POKÉMON ◉

Here's where you start, and these are the first
Pokémon you'll see in Kalos. Can you tell who
they are just by glimpsing their shadows?

1

2

3

ANSWER ON PAGE 111

KANTO

JOHTO

HOENN

SINNOH

UNOVA

KALOS

PUZZLER

The mysterious disappearance of Pokémon adventurers comes to a conclusion—they were all seeking mysterious Pokémon, but they could never finish the job. Here's the last cryptic clue left by one such traveler. What Pokémon did this explorer see before vanishing? Use page 101 for help.

During the new  __ __ __ __ ,

the eerie  __ __ __ __

of the  __ __ __ __ __ __ __ __ __

echoes through town, bringing  __ __ __

to anyone who  __ __ __ __ __ it.

KANTO

JOHTO

HOENN

SINNOH

UNOVA

KALOS

WEIGHT FOR IT

Avalugg somehow found itself perched on the edge of a roof, balancing precariously on a wooden beam. A few Pokémon friends showed up to help balance the beam out so Avalugg can walk on to an adjoining roof. Which of these Pokémon teams could balance out the beam without tipping it too far? You should come within 10 pounds of Avalugg's weight.

1,113.3 lbs.

TEAM 1

496.0 lbs.

TEAM 2

672.4 lbs.

TEAM 3

331.8 lbs.

474.0 lbs.

447.5 lbs.

595.2 lbs.

EVOLUTION REVOLUTION

You know your first partner Pokémon, but do you know their Evolutions? See if you can guess the correct order and fill in the numbers and names below.

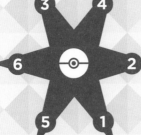

3 4
6 2
5 1

Chespin → (2)_____ → (2)_____
Fennekin → (8)_____ → (3)_____
Froakie → (4)_____ → ( )_____

ANSWER ON PAGE 111

KANTO

JOHTO

HOENN

SINNOH

UNOVA

KALOS

WHO'S THAT POKÉMON?

For the last time, let's see how good you are at spotting Pokémon on the fly. Can you match these Pokémon with their silhouettes on the left?

1

2

3

4

5

6

BUNNELBY

LITLEO

SCATTERBUG

FLABÉBÉ

SKIDDO

PANGORO

KANTO
JOHTO
HOENN
SINNOH
UNOVA
KALOS

KALOS CROSSWORD

A high level of intelligence is a sign of a regional specialist. Let's test your skills at knowing everything you can about Pokémon in Kalos.

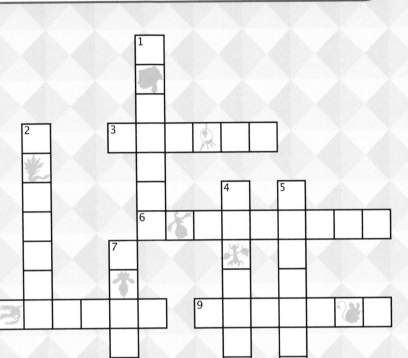

DOWN

1. Its broad, flat back is a common resting place for groups of Bergmite. Its big, bulky body can crush obstacles in its path.

2. _ _ _ _ _ _ _ dwells deep within a cave in the Kalos region. It is said that this Legendary Pokémon is a guardian of the ecosystem.

4. Using its roots, _ _ _ _ _ _ , _ _ _ can control the trees around it to protect its forest home. Smaller Pokémon sometimes live in its hollow body.

5. This Pokémon's horns shine in all the colors of the rainbow. It is said that this Legendary Pokémon can share the gift of endless life.

7. According to myth, when Carbink suddenly transforms into _ _ _ _ _ _ _ , its dazzling appearance is the most beautiful sight in existence. It has the power to compress carbon from the atmosphere, forming diamonds between its hands.

ACROSS

3. To keep valuables locked up tight, give the key to this Pokémon. This Pokémon loves to collect keys, and it will guard its collection with all its might.

6. During the new moon, the eerie song of the _ _ _ _ _ _ _ _ _ echoes through town, bringing woe to anyone who hears it.

8. When this Pokémon spreads its dark wings, its feathers give off a red glow. It is said that this Legendary Pokémon can absorb the life energy of others.

9. It uses its whiskers like antennas to communicate over long distances using electrical waves. It can soak up electricity through its tail.

10. They are masters when it comes to battling in the dark. The ultrasonic waves they release from their ears are powerful enough to crush a boulder.

KANTO

JOHTO

HOENN

SINNOH

UNOVA

KALOS

⊙ IT TAKES ALL TYPES ⊙

You know your region, and you seem to know your Pokémon, so let's see if you know your Pokémon types. Match the Pokémon on the left with the types on the right. Be careful—some of the Pokémon are dual types.

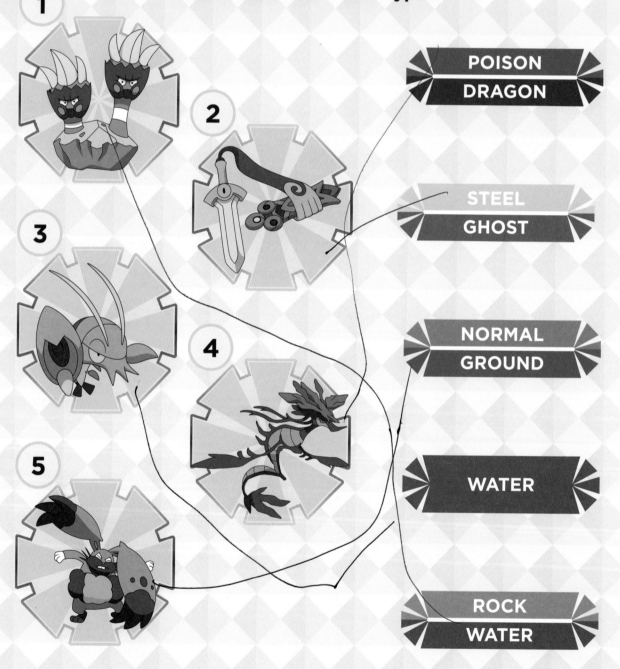

1

2

3

4

5

POISON
DRAGON

STEEL
GHOST

NORMAL
GROUND

WATER

ROCK
WATER

KANTO

JOHTO

HOENN

SINNOH

UNOVA

KALOS

MAZE ME

Here's a tough one. This super maze requires you to get Scatterbug to the middle, where a Spewpa is waiting for it. Then the both of you should get to Vivillon before it flies away. Hurry—you have less than 90 seconds to get to Vivillon before it flies off.

START

FINISH

KANTO

JOHTO

HOENN

SINNOH

UNOVA

KALOS

POKÉMON POETRY

**Being a regional specialist isn't all work—
sometimes you have to let your creative side shine.
Try to figure out which Pokémon fits in which
poem from some of the best bards in Kalos.**

From its claws it shoots water, a real hydro launcher
Knocking Pokémon from the air,
and its name is _Clawncher_

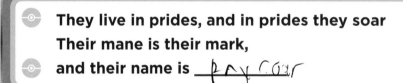

When you hear its eerie song, your nerves will be iced
It plays during a new moon, and it's called _Gourgeist_

They live in prides, and in prides they soar
Their mane is their mark,
and their name is _Pyroar_

It will read your mind when on its back you float
But those horns also lead the Pokémon _Gogoat_

Membranes cover its eyes like the face of a clock
Between Sandile and Krookodile
lies the wily _____

ANSWER ON PAGE 111

WORD SEARCH

The last chance to show off your regional expertise. Identify 71 of the new Kalos Pokémon in this word search, but watch out for Pokémon from Unova that may have crept in here!

```
F L E T C H L I N G U V X G D I A N C I E R P Z T
L R P A N C H A M B E R G M I T E C F B S F H Y A
E X O N G O G O A T C L A U N C H E R R W L A G L
T S J G P Y R O A R C H E S P I N X S A I O N A O
C L A E A R C A N I N E S Y L V E O N I R E T R N
H I M L P D W Z F H G O U R G E I S T X L T U D F
I G A A Y N I N E T A L E S K R E L P E I T M E L
N G U D L O H E L I O P T I L E Q Z P N X E P C A
D O R N O I V E R N O D L N D I G G E R S B Y F M
E O A H O O P A T R E V E N A N T G L B G N V E E
R Q A R O M A T I S S E U E C C Y R I Z O T E N A
E U E U S P E W P A D J S W R A O E T L O Y L N V
S I G B R E M A L A M A R V K L T N L R D R T E A
P L I I S O R E L M E G V N T N I I E W R A A K L
U L S N S J R B O N X E I H U E V N O N A N L I U
R A L A K Y U U R W G K G R I I O J G M A T O N G
R D A C I O L E S L S U Y K V S C A T T E R B U G
F I S L D Y X Y A I A T A D E L P H O X O U Y D E
L N H E D I B G L N A O I M S U S U P G L M Q E N
A U Q N O L A O S D R L V C A R B I N K O H Z D O
B B E K E R I E O F C K P U M P K A B O O T G E I
É X L N D L H O N E D G E H E U P H G S I P A N B
B R N C E C L A W I T Z E R R F U R F R O U Y N A
É U O H A W L U C H A O K L E F K I P T E U F E T
B A R B A R A C L E X F L O R G E S A W S B U C K
```

KANTO

JOHTO

HOENN

SINNOH

UNOVA

KALOS

KANTO
JOHTO
HOENN
SINNOH
UNOVA
KALOS

PARTS NOT INCLUDED

Some Pokémon move very quickly, and you may just catch a glimpse of them. Match the Kalos Pokémon to its appendages, and gather some experience for your certificate!

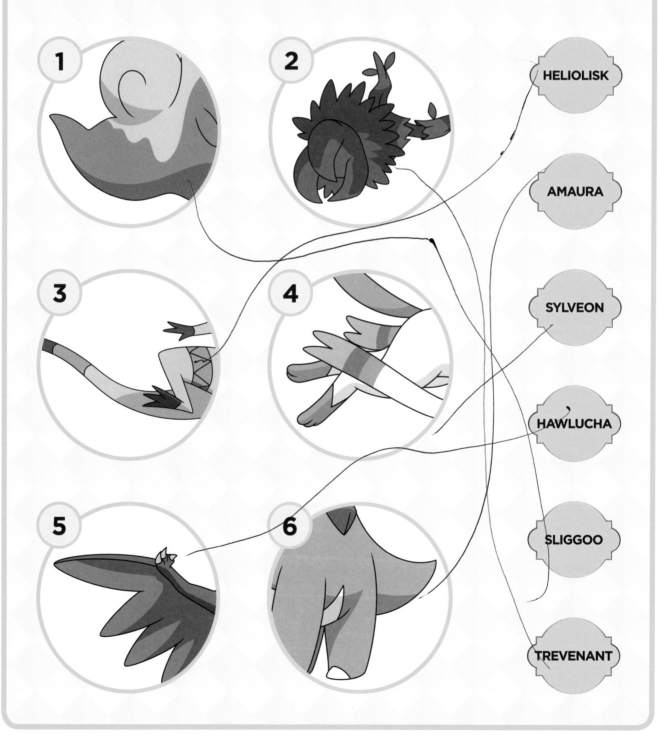

1

2

3

4

5

6

HELIOLISK

AMAURA

SYLVEON

HAWLUCHA

SLIGGOO

TREVENANT

KANTO

JOHTO

HOENN

SINNOH

UNOVA

KALOS

POKÉMON ACROSTICS

Let's see how much you know about mixing up the Kalos Pokémon names. Play this game with one, two, or three players.

RULES

Pick a Pokémon name. Write that name in a column. If you pick a Pokémon like Aromatisse, you should have a puzzle that looks like this. Now, try to spell the longest word you can with the letters in each row. For example, starting with the first letter, try to spell the longest word you can with "a", like "advertisement." You can only make one word per row, but you get a point for each letter in the word.

A _____

R _____

O _____

M _____

A _____

T _____

I _____

S _____

S _____

E _____

 BONUS Time the game and see how many words you can make in two minutes. Give yourself an extra five points per line for spelling Pokémon names!

KANTO

JOHTO

HOENN

SINNOH

UNOVA

KALOS

WALL SCRAWL

Wait a minute—maybe the mystery isn't over yet! Another intrepid traveler has left behind clues about Pokémon they've sighted. See if you can tell which Pokémon they are!

1 A ROME A TEASE

2 BYE NUCK ELL

3 DIH GURZ BEE

4 SWUR LICKS

5 DRUH GAL JEE

6 DEH DEN NAY

7 CLOW IT ZUR

8 QWILL UH DINN

9 FRO GA DEER

10 TREV UH NONT

ANSWER ON PAGE 112

END OF THE LINE

Finally, you have come to the end of your journey so far. You've done a great job of identifying and locating almost every Pokémon there is! Now let's see if you can pick out the last Evolutions of the first partner Pokémon from page 86 mixed in with these other Kalos Pokémon.

KANTO
JOHTO
HOENN
SINNOH
UNOVA
KALOS

Certificate of Completion

This is to certify that

_____

has achieved the rank of Pokémon regional specialist for the region of Kalos.

FROAKIE

CHESPIN

FENNEKIN

FROGADIER

QUILLADIN

BRAIXEN

GRENINJA

CHESNAUGHT

DELPHOX

Issued this _____ day of _____, 20 __

PUZZLERS KEY

 A

 B

 C

D

 E

 F

 G

 H

 I

 J

 K

 L

 M

 N

 O

 P

 Q

 R

 S

 T

 U

 V

 W

 X

 Y

Z

KANTO
JOHTO
HOENN
SINNOH
UNOVA
KALOS

KANTO
JOHTO
HOENN
SINNOH
UNOVA
KALOS

BONUS MEGA MATCHUP

During your journey through the regions you found some curious stones. These are Mega Stones, which are used during battle to temporarily transform Pokémon. But only specific Pokémon matched with their specific Mega Stone can make the change occur! Connect the Pokémon from each of the regions with their specific Mega Stone and their Mega-Evolved Pokémon by drawing lines to each. Only the very best Trainers are up to this task!

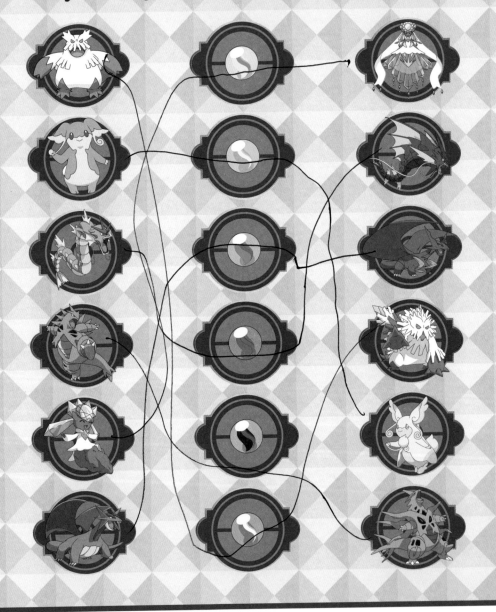

ANSWER KEY

If you've made it to the answer key, congratulations! That means you have challenged yourself to become a true Pokémon specialist by completing your training activities. Good job! And if you're still in training, then remember, only look at the answers for the training activities you have finished.

PAGE 6

1) Bulbasaur

2) Squirtle

3) Charmander

PAGE 7

K A B U T O P S J S L O W B R O R M E M A G I K A R P E W E A V V
A I S I Q P R I M E A P E T V F A R F E T C H D A F L P D P B A I
N P N D I T T O C L O Y S T E R T M L W V S N G V T Y O V U R C L
G O O M M S L O W P O K E S N S T I N C X E N D R E R R U H A A T
A M R S H E L L D E R G O U C A M G D E E B O G G Y L I T M A K O
S F L M A G N E T O N O I X S Y T E D D G T T D C F R G P I A R R
K L A H D P R Q I T R M A T A O L N U R I E L X I M G O K A Z E Y
H A X C I R M A K S D Y S Q U H O I C A P L V Q R M N X O G A A D
A R W H T A W O A O J T S R R E G Z G W E E P I N B E L L N L M E
N E E O M T D L O E W G O N G R E G D I G L O O M K R A O C Y E L
E O S P O I K B U T T E R F R E E R A G F E A R O W N D R H P W H
K N E T I N N U E G O L B A T W X A Q C G W C S H Y E Y E A A U T
A P A K D G E J I L X L W F N Z Z E Z E T S L F T C O N H L N E N F W A
N S N I E E W A B K T M S T A R M I E N N T M B B C N R I M A N K E Y
G S A S I N O W G S A A G F P A J N H G G F U A X N O R R Z A P D O S
R I G T E P A O U F A H R O T A G E L F C Z K D P O L I W H I R L
O R D T O Y I L R B O A R D R U N T A R C A N I N E G O L E M U M
W C T L K C V I R S M G A A S S T O R A B M D U G T R I O E R H A
L L E F R Y A U R A O B T H E R B A P P T P A R A S E C T C G N O
I F R Y S A I I H S N B E R A O G I P O N Y T A A W D T N E D A
T H A M A G N A L O N A T I Y R E K Z K C O L A W G T O O W W E M
H E A V A U R N M C E N S K A T B P W C A T R I V W N E P O E S C T
A R E G R O A U A O P A A Y E W C P O W G E M A R Q E B I T Y L L
R Y L M G V D D E N W L E N N Y C E H E W R T L T A O L D A R T O
H Y H R R O A B P A L T R O D I S U O D I J A D U R Z A O E P A M L R E T Z U
H O D D G N P L A S A U D O S E B L O Y R I E H S N E T T Y N I C U B
O H P O A E M P H M O L T R E S S A O P A L S U N X W A Z D C S C
R S N V M K X C X O C L E F A B L E S U N S L D R A I C H U Z A C T
N E E R A P I D A S H K A K U N A F A H E O N I D O R I N O N C
V J A E S Q U I R T L E J O L T E O N D V E N O M O T H M A O Z K
J H P N L R A T I C A T E Y P W O O P E R F N J U M P L U F F L C
C H A R M A N D E R U Z U O K O F F I N G A S T L Y O M A N Y T E

PAGE 8

1) Eevee:
Normal

2) Farfetch'd:
Normal/Flying

3) Slowpoke:
Water/Psychic

4) Gengar:
Ghost/Poison

5) Gyarados:
Water/Flying

PAGE 9

Bulbasaur ➜ (4) Ivysaur ➜ (3) Venusaur
Charmander ➜ (6) Charmeleon ➜ (1) Charizard
Squirtle ➜ (2) Wartortle ➜ (5) Blastoise

KANTO

JOHTO

HOENN

SINNOH

UNOVA

KALOS

PAGE 10

Crossword solution:

```
 ¹H        ²M A N K E Y
  Y         A
 ³P S Y D U C K      ⁴K O F F I N G   ⁵G
  N         H       ⁶A              E
  O         O        L              O
            P       ⁷P I K A C ⁸H U  D
            K           K    O       U
            A           A    R       D
            Z          ⁹S H E L L D E R
            A               S
            M               E
            M               A
```

PAGE 11

Team 2

Weedle   **Onix**

Kangaskhan

PAGE 12

Exeggutor   **Primeape**

Golem   **Oddish**   **Weedle**

PAGE 13

1) Dugtrio   2) Paras

3) Raichu   4) Vulpix

5) Rattata   6) Beedrill

PAGE 14

1) Mr. Mime   2) Magmar

3) Dewgong   4) Seaking

5) Growlithe   6) Tauros

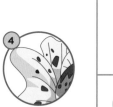

PAGE 15

4) Vaporeon

PAGE 16

This **LEGENDARY** Pokémon often brings **SNOWFALL** in its wake. When **ARTICUNO** flaps its wings, the **AIR** turns chilly.

PAGE 17

PAGE 18

Mewtwo

PAGE 19

Charizard

Blastoise   Venusaur

PAGE 22

1) Cyndaquil

2) Chikorita

3) Totodile

PAGE 23

Blissey

Tyrogue

Shuckle

PAGE 24

1) Stantler

 2) Crobat

 3) Mantine

 4) Chinchou

 5) Ledyba

 6) Ursaring

 7) Flaaffy

PAGE 25

Chikorita ➡ (3) Bayleef ➡ (2) Meganium
Cyndaquil ➡ (4) Quilava ➡ (1) Typhlosion
Totodile ➡ (6) Croconaw ➡ (5) Feraligatr

PAGE 26

1) Wobbuffet: Psychic

2) Houndoom: Dark/Fire

3) Pichu: Electric

4) Sudowoodo: Rock

5) Togepi: Fairy

6) Smeargle: Normal

PAGE 27

Tyranitar

PAGE 28

Legend says their **FEATHERS** bring joy to whoever holds one. When **HO-OH**'s feathers catch the light at different angles, they glow in a **RAINBOW** of colors.

PAGE 29

1 Skiploom

2 Qwilfish

3 Porygon 2

4 Dunsparce

5 Scizor

6 Remoraid

PAGE 30

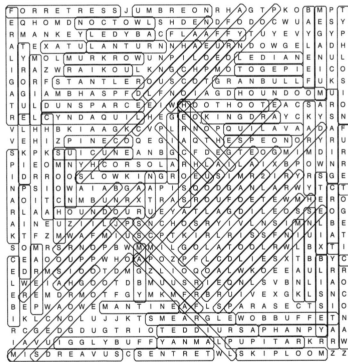

PAGE 31

(Crossword) ²SKARMORY · ³HERACROSS · ⁷UNOWN · ⁹CELEBI · ¹⁰ENTEI

PAGE 33

4) Pineco

PAGE 34

PAGE 35

Meganium   Feraligatr   Typhlosion

KANTO

JOHTO

HOENN

SINNOH

UNOVA

KALOS

PAGE 38

1) Treecko

2) Mudkip

3) Torchic

PAGE 39

1) Wailord: Water

2) Sableye:
Dark/Ghost

3) Mightyena:
Dark

4) Tropius:
Grass/Flying

5) Mawile:
Steel/Fairy

6) Minun:
Electric

PAGE 40

4) Armaldo

PAGE 41

Treecko ➜ (4) Grovyle ➜ (6) Sceptile
Torchic ➜ (1) Combusken ➜ (2) Blaziken
Mudkip ➜ (3) Marshtomp ➜ (5) Swampert

PAGE 42

Flygon

PAGE 44

1) Solrock: Rock Polish

2) Lombre: Water Sport

3) Glalie: Ice Fang

4) Kecleon: Tail Whip

PAGE 45

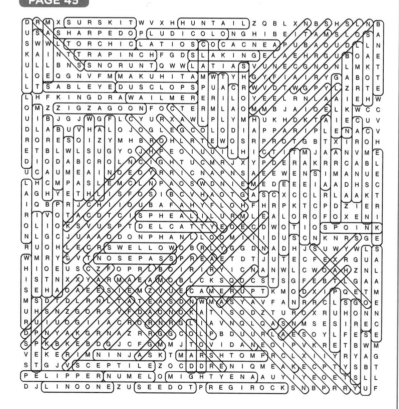

PAGE 46

Dear Diary,
Minerals from the <u>ROCKS</u>
become part of its gemstone <u>EYES</u>
and the <u>CRYSTALS</u> on its body.
<u>SABLEYE</u> lives deep in
a <u>CAVE</u> where it uses its
sharp <u>CLAWS</u> to dig up rocks
for <u>FOOD</u>.

KANTO

JOHTO

HOENN

SINNOH

UNOVA

KALOS

PAGE 47

```
    ¹G              ²J I ²R A C H I
     R               E
     O       ⁴L      G
⁵R A Y Q U A Z A    ⁶R E G I R O C K  ⁷K
     D       T       G               Y
     O       I       I               O
     N       ⁸L A T I O S            G
             S       T               R
                     E               E
                     ⁹D E O X Y S
                     L
```

PAGE 49

PAGE 48

1) Nosepass

2) Lunatone

3) Vigoroth

4) Salamence

5) Masquerain

6) Kyogre

7) Hariyama

8) Sealeo

9) Wynaut

10) Corphish

PAGE 50

1) Dustox

2) Delcatty

3) Exploud

4) Banette

5) Breloom

6) Shiftry

PAGE 51

Swampert

Blaziken

Sceptile

PAGE 54

1) Chimchar

2) Piplup

3) Turtwig

PAGE 55

1) Magnezone

2) Croagunk

3) Buizel

4) Vespiquen

5) Chatot

6) Pachirisu

PAGE 57

Turtwig ➜ (3) Grotle ➜ (2) Torterra
Chimchar ➜ (4) Monferno ➜ (5) Infernape
Piplup ➜ (6) Prinplup ➜ (1) Empoleon

PAGE 58

GASTRODON

PAGE 59

1) Burmy: Bug

2) Spiritomb: Ghost/Dark

3) Lucario: Fighting/Steel

4) Glameow: Normal

5) Carnivine: Grass

4) Gallade: Psychic/Fighting

PAGE 60

Rampardos 226.0 lbs.   Bronzor 133.4 lbs.   Munchlax 231.5 lbs.

Kricketot 4.9 lbs.   Shinx 20.9 lbs.   Burmy 7.5 lbs.

PAGE 61

3) Ambipom

PAGE 62

They are all Grass type, except for Roserade, which is Grass/Poison.

PAGE 63

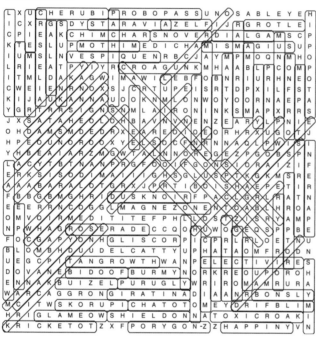

PAGE 64

They take **FLIGHT** at **DUSK**, but since they can't control their direction, they'll drift away wherever the **WIND** blows them. During the day, **DRIFBLIM** tend to be **SLEEPY**.

PAGE 65

PAGE 66

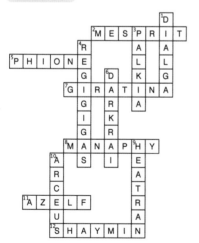

PAGE 67

Infernape   Torterra   Empoleon

PAGE 70

1) Tepig

2) Snivy

3) Oshawott

PAGE 71

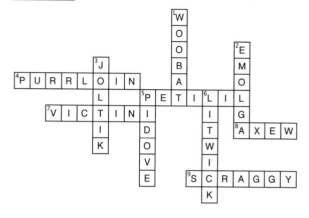

Crossword answers:
- 1 (down) WOOBAT
- 2 (down) EMOLGA
- 3 (down) JELLICENT... JLTIK (JOLTIK)
- 4 (across) PURRLOIN
- 5 (across) PETILIL
- 6 (down) LITWICK
- 7 (across) VICTINI
- 8 (across) AXEW
- 9 (across) SCRAGGY
- (down) IDOVE (KILDOVE/PIDOVE)

PAGE 72

1) Minccino

2) Munna

4) Yamask

3) Trubbish

6) Tynamo

5) Sigilyph

7) Deerling

PAGE 73

Snivy ➜ (5) Servine ➜ (1) Serperior
Tepig ➜ (6) Pignite ➜ (4) Emboar
Oshawott ➜ (3) Dewott ➜ (2) Samurott

PAGE 75

LEGENDS tell of a time when this Pokémon attacked a mighty CASTLE to protect its Pokémon friends. THEY say it knocked down a GIANT wall with the FORCE of its charge. I saw a TERRAKION!

PAGE 76

2) Braviary

PAGE 74

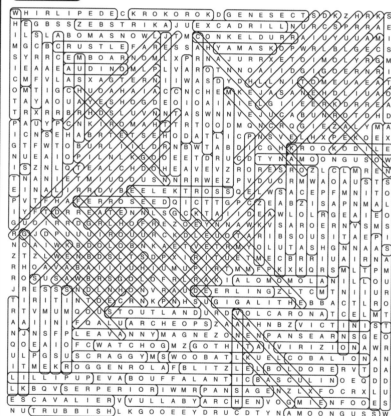

KANTO

JOHTO

HOENN

SINNOH

UNOVA

KALOS

KANTO

JOHTO

HOENN

SINNOH

UNOVA

KALOS

PAGE 77

PAGE 78

1

Carracosta

2

Beartic

3

Vanillish

4

Ferrothorn

5

Haxorus

6

Eelektrik

PAGE 79

Jellicent
297.6 lbs.

Timburr
27.6 lbs.

Bisharp
154.3 lbs.

Genesect
181.9 lbs.

Mienfoo
44.1 lbs.

Purrloin
22.3 lbs.

PAGE 81

Heatmor

Mienshao

Haxorus

Bouffalant

Zoroark

PAGE 82

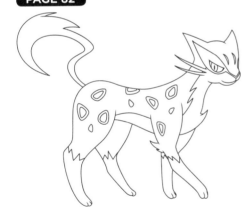

PAGE 83

Serperior

Samurott

Emboar

PAGE 86

1) Chespin

2) Fennekin

3) Froakie

PAGE 87

During the new **MOON**, the eerie **SONG** of the **GOURGEIST** echoes through town, bringing **WOE** to anyone who **HEARS** it.

PAGE 88

Team 2

Zygarde

Yveltal

PAGE 89

Chespin ➜ (2) Quilladin ➜ (6) Chesnaught
Fennekin ➜ (5) Braixen ➜ (3) Delphox
Froakie ➜ (4) Frogadier ➜ (1) Greninja

PAGE 90

1) Litleo

2) Flabébé

3) Skiddo

4) Scatterbug

5) Bunnelby

6) Pangoro

PAGE 91

Crossword answers:

```
            ¹A
            V
            A
  ²Z    ³K L E F K I
  Y      U
  G      G        ⁴T    ⁵X
  A      ⁶G O U R G E I S T
  R      ⁷D       E      R
  D      I        V      N
⁸Y V E L T A L    ⁹D E D E N N E
         N        N      A
         C        A      S
       ¹⁰N O I V E R N T
         E
```

PAGE 92

1) Binacle: Rock/Water

2) Honedge: Steel/Ghost

3) Clauncher: Water

4) Dragalge: Poison/Dragon

5) Diggersby: Normal/Ground

PAGE 93

PAGE 94

Clauncher

Gourgeist

Pyroar

Gogoat

Krokorok

KANTO

JOHTO

HOENN

SINNOH

UNOVA

KALOS

PAGE 95

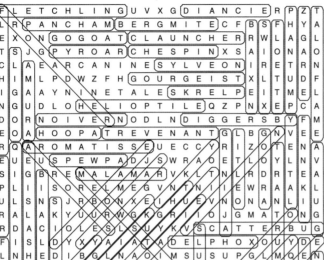

```
F L E T C H L I N G U V X G D I A N C I E R P Z T
L R P A N C H A M B E R G M I T E C F B S F H A N
E X O N G O G O A T C L A U N C H E R R W L A G L
T C S J G P Y R O A R C H E S P I N X S A I O E A
C L A E A R C A N I N E S Y L V E O N I R E T R T
H I M L P D W Z F H G O U R G E I S T X L T U D I
I G A A Y N I N E T A L E S K R E L P E I T M E O
N D U D L O H E L I O P T I L E Q Z P N X E P R N
G O R A N O I V E R N O D L N D I G G E R S B Y F
D R A H O O P A T R E V E N A N T G L B G N V E A
E Q A R O M A T I S S E U E C C Y R I Z O T E N M
R U E U S P E W P A D J S W R A O E T L O Y L N E
E I G B R E M A L A M A R V K L T N L R D R T E A
S L S I S O R E L M E G V N T N I I E W R A K L V
P A N A S J R B O N X E I H U E V O N A N A L I A
U D A C Y U U R W G K G R I O J G M A T O N G N L
R I L A L O L E S L S U Y K V S C A T T E R B U G
R N H E D Y X Y A I A T A D E L P H O X O U Y D E
F A E D I B G L N A O I M S U S U P G L M Q E N N
L U Q N O L A O S D R L V C A R B I N K O H Z D O
A B E K E R I E O F C K P U M P K A B O O T G E I
B X L N D L H O N E D G E H E U P H G S I P A N E
R N C E C L A W I T Z E R R F U R F R O U Y N N B
E U O H A W L U C H A O K L E F K I P T E U F E T
B A R B A R A C L E X F L O R G E S A W S B U C K
```

PAGE 96

1

Sliggoo

2

Trevenant

3

Heliolisk

4

Sylveon

5

Hawlucha

6

Amaura

PAGE 98

1) Aromatisse

2) Binacle

3) Diggersby

4) Swirlix

5) Dragalge

6) Dedenne

7) Clawitzer

8) Quilladin

9) Frogadier

10) Trevanant

PAGE 99

Chesnaught

Delphox

Greninja

BONUS MEGA MATCHUP PAGE 102

KANTO
 + =
Gyarados **Gyaradosite** **Mega Gyarados**

JOHTO
 + =
Tyranitar **Tyranitarite** **Mega Tyranitar**

HOENN
 +  =
Salamence **Salamencite** **Mega Salamence**

SINNOH
 +  =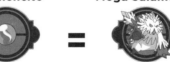
Abomasnow **Abomasite** **Mega Abomasnow**

UNOVA
 +  =
Audino **Audinite** **Mega Audino**

KALOS
 + =
Diancie **Diancite** **Mega Diancie**